No Longer Just a Dream

His eyes were blue.

Christine hadn't expected that. She'd just assumed they would be brown, in fact, dark brown. An illogical conclusion to have jumped to, she realized, since she had never met the man.

Well, yes and no.

Only moments ago he had been making love to her in her "waking" dream, and she swore she could still taste him on her lips, smell him on her skin, feel him move inside of her. No wonder she was disconcerted. And a little embarrassed. She knew who he was, of course. She'd caught an occasional glimpse of him in newspapers and magazines, although she had to admit those photographs had not done him justice.

The man was Adrian King: multimillionaire—billionaire, some speculated—although no one seemed to know for certain how much wealth he'd managed to accumulate since he had arrived on the scene, taking Las Vegas by storm. Whatever his background Adrian King exuded power as if it were his birthright, as if it had permeated his heart and mind and soul, even his skin, for thousands of years.

Christine took an involuntary step toward him. There was something about Adrian King that drew her in, mesmerized her without a word, with only a glance.

The word *warrior* popped into Christine's head, and she remembered another time when that description had been applied to a man, a very special man.

⚦NIGHT LIFE⚦

ELIZABETH GUEST

BERKLEY SENSATION, NEW YORK

THE BERKLEY PUBLISHING GROUP
Published by the Penguin Group
Penguin Group (USA) Inc.
375 Hudson Street, New York, New York 10014, USA
Penguin Group (Canada), 90 Eglinton Avenue East, Suite 700, Toronto, Ontario M4P 2Y3, Canada
(a division of Pearson Penguin Canada Inc.)
Penguin Books Ltd., 80 Strand, London WC2R 0RL, England
Penguin Group Ireland, 25 St. Stephen's Green, Dublin 2, Ireland (a division of Penguin Books Ltd.)
Penguin Group (Australia), 250 Camberwell Road, Camberwell, Victoria 3124, Australia
(a division of Pearson Australia Group Pty. Ltd.)
Penguin Books India Pvt. Ltd., 11 Community Centre, Panchsheel Park, New Delhi—110 017, India
Penguin Group (NZ), 67 Apollo Drive, Mairangi Bay, Auckland 1311, New Zealand
(a division of Pearson New Zealand Ltd.)
Penguin Books (South Africa) (Pty.) Ltd., 24 Sturdee Avenue, Rosebank, Johannesburg 2196,
South Africa

Penguin Books Ltd., Registered Offices: 80 Strand, London WC2R 0RL, England

This is a work of fiction. Names, characters, places, and incidents either are the product of the author's imagination or are used fictitiously, and any resemblance to actual persons, living or dead, business establishments, events, or locales is entirely coincidental. The publisher does not have any control over and does not assume any responsibility for author or third-party websites or their content.

NIGHT LIFE

A Berkley Sensation Book / published by arrangement with the author

PRINTING HISTORY
Berkley Prime Crime mass-market edition / April 2007

Copyright © 2007 by Suzanne Simmons Guntrum.
Cover photo by Ron Zinn.
Cover design by Judy York.
Interior text design by Kristin del Rosario.

ISBN: 978-0-425-21482-4

BERKLEY SENSATION®
Berkley Sensation Books are published by The Berkley Publishing Group,
a division of Penguin Group (USA) Inc.,
375 Hudson Street, New York, New York 10014.
BERKLEY SENSATION is a registered trademark of Penguin Group (USA) Inc.
The "B" design is a trademark belonging to Penguin Group (USA) Inc.

PRINTED IN THE UNITED STATES OF AMERICA

10 9 8 7 6 5 4 3 2 1

For Ray, always.

And for Jayne Ann Krentz,
because she always believed.
Without her encouragement,
I might never have written Seti's story.

"Where have all the good men gone
and where are all the gods?"
  —"Holding Out for a Hero"

"I have in me something dangerous."
  —*Hamlet*

PROLOGUE

Thebes
1192 B.C.E.

He was dying.

Merneptah Seti could feel the life force within him slowly slipping away as surely as the precious fluids of his body would seep from his quick to putrefy flesh once he breathed his last breath. With one final spasm his sphincter would release its grip, his bowels would open wide like the lotus flower unfolding its perfumed petals to the warmth of the morning sun, the ensuing gush of human excrement defiling the fine linen of his bed, the sharp ammoniacal smell of urine—the "salt of Amon"—filling the palace room in which he lay. The stink of death would soon follow.

Seti knew what would come after. He remembered well the seventy days of preparations that speeded his father on his way to the other side of the River of Life, the Nile.

Ritual had long prescribed what must be done to preserve the king's body. He would be taken to the awaiting *wabet* and *per-nefer*, and the mortuary priests would wash him in a purifying stream of water. After the anointing of his head and body, the first of the royal embalming priests, wearing the jackal-headed mask of the god Anubis, would insert a chisel into his nostrils and break through the septum and bony wall into his brain. The useless gray matter—although there were those who believed it was this very matter that gave men, and gods, their intelligence, their spirit, their power, and not the heart as was commonly held to be true—this now lifeless food for maggots would be extracted by means of an iron probe with a scoop on one end.

Next, his head would be tilted back and a caustic would be poured into the nearly empty vessel, and when the remaining tissue that clung to the inside of his cranium was liquefied, it would flow from his nostrils, soft and gray and foul smelling. Finally, his hollow skull would be stuffed with linen steeped in resin, his ears, his nostril holes, even the empty sockets of his sightless eyes.

Chanting the rituals of his father and his father's father and his father's father before him, the embalmer would take up the sharp Ethiopian stone and slice through his pelvis, cutting diagonally from his hip bone toward the pubic area, taking great care not to damage the penis or the testicles.

Surely he would have need of his genitalia in the afterlife as he had in this life, Seti thought with a sardonic smile upon his lips.

Next, the viscera would be wrested from his body,

innards removed, treated and placed in their appropriate canopic jars, which would then be stored for all eternity in four miniature gold coffins, to be watched over by the four sons of Horus: the god Imset to guard his liver; the baboon-headed god Hapy, his lungs; Qebhsenuef, the falcon, his intestines; and the god Duwamutef, his stomach.

By all the demons that dwelled in the Underworld, by the Eater of Blood and the Breaker of Bones, he was to be carved up into bits and pieces like a sacrificial animal, like the young calf whose leg would be amputated while it still lived, its bawl of pain renting the air around the burial tomb as its blood splattered the priest-butcher's white tunic, as a river of red soaked into the hot desert sands. The calf would be sacrificed so that he, the mighty king, might live again and forever.

Seti trembled. Sour-tasting bile rose from his gut and settled in the back of his parched throat. Fear, awful fear, fear greater than any he had ever known in battle, suddenly clouded his heart.

What if he were not a god after all, but a man like any other man? How could his internal organs somehow magically be restored to him? How could life stir once again in the gutted cavity of his body? How could he speak or hear or smell or taste or feel when he would be stuffed and trussed like a succulent partridge served at a celebratory banquet?

Was he man or god?

They said he was god on the day of his coronation in the last year of his father's reign. They said he was god in the many temples that bore his name and in the palace that served as his golden cage, watched over by servant and slave alike.

Seti slowly opened his eyes. They were all there waiting for a word, a look, a movement of his royal hand: Mererwikair, who served as his vizier and who had served as his father's before him; Thutnefer, the aged chancellor, bent with rheumatism but with a heart as cunning and as dangerous as the Nile crocodile; Menna, the chief steward; Ranefer, the priest-physician, with his jars of evil-tasting potions and evil-smelling poultices; Memi, the chief scribe; Rahotep, his greatest general; and last, his half-brother, Prince Rekhmire.

Seti sighed and closed his eyes again. Perhaps it was better to cross over into the next life now, he thought, while he was still endowed with physical strength and physical beauty, before his body betrayed him wholly, before he grew weak in mind and spirit and shriveled up into a feeble, pathetic old man.

Still, he was afraid of dying.

What was there to fear? According to the priests of Sekmet and those who served the gods at the Temple of Karnak, the afterlife promised to be all that this life had been and more. He would be free to indulge in the pleasures that were the king's due: eating the choicest meats, drinking the finest wines, playing hounds and jackals with the cleverest at his court, hunting the antelope, listening to the music of the harp and the lyre, watching the dancers as their nude bodies swayed seductively in time to the music.

His palace in the next life would be as magnificent as any palace ever constructed. There was to be a throne room of mammoth proportions in which he would hold court and counsel as he did in this life. The living quarters would include a long-columned hall lined with royal suites on either side and, at one end, his own lavish apartments.

In that mortuary palace, intended to serve as his eternal home, murals would abound as they did in all his palaces up and down the Nile. Wooden columns, richly ornamented with paintings of the papyrus and the lotus, symbolizing Lower and Upper Egypt; larger-than-life figures of himself, his wives, his children, even his dear Mui, earthly representation of the cat goddess Bastet, would cover the plastered brick walls. The sky, complete with carved birds and insects, would be illustrated on the ceiling, watched over by the goddess Nut, and the floor would simulate a pond teeming with fish and fowl.

Seti thought of his first wife and chief queen, Nefertari, named for that most favored wife of the Great Ramses. Their marriage, like so many royal marriages, had been one of political gain and political necessity: an alliance of two great Egyptian families.

Betrothed when he was but nine and she eight, they eventually had four children together before she had grown ill from the strange fever at the time of the Inundation and had died. He had grown fond of Nefertari during their years together, and he had missed her companionship after she was gone.

Still, no woman, not even Nefertari, had found that most favored place in his heart and mind and soul. Perhaps he was destined to be alone, lonely, throughout eternity.

Then he thought of the woman, the beautiful stranger, who sometimes appeared to him while he slept. He'd told no one of her, or of his dreams, although dreams were said to be messages from the gods and needed interpretation by his counselors. After all, even a king—especially a king—was entitled to his secrets.

She was his secret. He welcomed the night and the dreams it promised, because of her. He had once concocted a special perfume for her, made from the finest oils and the rarest scents. He had even written a love poem in her honor.

Perhaps it wouldn't be so bad to cross into the afterlife if he knew that this long-anticipated lover would be there waiting for him. No woman would ever be her equal, not in beauty, nor grace, nor intelligence. None could capture his heart as she could.

"You're a fool," Seti said in a whisper so that none of those present could hear him. She wasn't real. She didn't exist. She was created from his own imagination and from his loneliness. There was no perfect woman for him.

Ma'ya. The scent of her reached his nostrils first. Amidst the burning incense and the priest-physician's unsavory concoction of testicles-of-a-black-ass, donkey's dung, and milk-of-a-woman-who-has-borne-a-son, she was as a garland of freshly gathered flowers.

"Divine one," she said softly.

Seti made a slight acknowledgment.

Ma'ya drew closer, head bowed, eyes averted, displaying the proper obeisance as she approached him. She knelt and brushed her lips reverently across the hand that lay at his side. "O great king, I bow before thy strength and wisdom."

Seti tried to speak what was in his heart, but managed only to say, "Ma'ya."

"It is I, my lord," she intoned, bending near.

His throat was on fire. "Wine."

That quickly, there was a silver goblet in her hand. Waving the servants aside, she held it to his lips. He sipped. The sweet liquid ran down his throat, momentarily cooling the fire and easing the spasms in his belly.

Seti tried to move his legs and found it impossible. This accursed weakness in his limbs! Why didn't his priests and physicians know what ailed him? What made him, the strongest of men, the greatest of warriors, as weak as a babe? He was five and thirty: no longer young, but not yet old.

He itched from head to toe; his flesh seemed to be crawling with insects. "My skin . . ."

Ma'ya understood. She always did. He felt the touch of her hands moving over him as she carefully applied the rarest of the seven sacred oils. She allowed no one else the intimacy of performing this task for him.

Seti bade her come closer, then whispered in her ear, "Send them all away."

Ma'ya stood and faced the group of attending courtiers. "It is the king's wish that you shall depart and wait upon his counsel." Then she also dismissed the servants and slaves until it was only the two of them. Once they were alone, she knelt beside him and began again, lightly kneading the soothing unguent into his skin.

"Soon I will depart this life for the next." The words escaped Seti's lips on a mere thread of sound.

Ma'ya stopped and looked up into his face. "No."

His response was emphatic. "Yes."

"But thy priests and physicians have said thou art improving every day," she stated.

"My priests and physicians do not speak the truth. They say what they believe their god and king wants to hear."

"But thou art the greatest of all magicians. Thy power transcends that of mere mortal man. It is thee who makes the River of Life rise and fall each year. It is thee who imposes order and prevents chaos. It is thee who preserves the harmony of the universe. Surely this great power can be used to save thyself," she said.

"I do not think it is so." He watched as tears quickly formed in her eyes, and his heart was touched. "I shall miss thee, Ma'ya."

A hot tear dropped from her cheek onto his thigh, scalding his flesh. For a moment she did not dare look upon him. "I am thy loyal subject. Do not forsake me, mighty pharaoh, king of the North and the South, he who is one with Osiris, Lord of the Netherworld." Then she raised her eyes to his; they were outlined with kohl and appeared large and luminous in her face. "I am thy loving consort, Ma'ya. Leave me never, my lord," she pleaded eloquently.

"I'm afraid I must," he said.

The soft strands of her wig brushed against his leg. "Then I would comfort thee while I may," she offered.

Seti reached down and put his hand beneath her chin. "You may dance for me, Ma'ya."

"As you wish, divine one." She rose from her knees and began to disrobe. She took the boudoir slippers from her feet; they were fashioned from the softest antelope hides. Unhooking the amethyst brooch at her waist, she placed it on a nearby table. Her outer cloak and narrow, pleated, semitransparent dress of the finest white linen followed, then the crown she wore on her head: a circlet of delicate gold inlaid with turquoise and carnelian.

She stood before him wearing only the traditional black wig and an assortment of jewelry. Her almond-shaped eyes loomed large. Her lips and cheeks were colored with red ochre. She raised her hand and foot, and he could see that she had applied a small amount of henna to redden her palms and the soles of her feet, as was the custom.

From across the courtyard outside his palace bedroom the sound of a harp could be heard. Ma'ya paused for a moment and then began to dance. He watched as she moved gracefully around the floor. Her neck was long and elegant, and she wore a jeweled collar plate about her throat. Her breasts were small and firm, their nipples gilded with gold. At her wrists and ankles, silver bracelets tinkled in time to the harp music.

For a moment Seti floated on a memory of pure erotic pleasure. Or was it one of his dreams? He was once again in the exquisite garden at his palace at Tell-el-Dab. It was evening. The young woman, the beautiful stranger who came to him by night, was bathing in the dark blue waters of a courtyard pool. She beckoned to him and he rose from a stone bench, dropped the loincloth he wore, and waded into the water. Once he stood in the waist-deep pool, he pulled her toward him and speared her with his flesh. Like the Nile crocodile and its mate, Seti took her again and again in the ritual "water dance." And when he was finished, he lay back in the cool water and floated beside her.

Soon his body would be awash in another kind of bath, Seti thought. The royal embalming priests would lay him in the "bath of death," a tub of natron salts that would dry his flesh and leave him only shriveled skin and bone. He would be cleansed with palm oil and aromatic spices, then stuffed with more resin-soaked linen so that his remains might retain some of their original shape. They would pack his cheekbones, his torso, his genitalia, even his legs. His fingernails and toenails would be sewn to his withered flesh and capped with gold. Once his entire body had been treated, it would be coated with resin to keep out moisture and the stench of death and decay for all eternity, so it could be said of him: "Merneptah Seti doth contain such a sweet odor that he is the sweet-smelling soul of the great god, himself."

Reciting the incantations and magical spells that were to accompany each part of the ritual wrapping, the embalmers would continue their labors. Yards upon yards of specially woven bandages would be wound about him, bound so tightly that if he had somehow miraculously survived at that point he would have been suffocated by them, buried alive in fine white pharaoh's linen.

Suddenly overcome by his own inability to breathe, Seti began to gasp for air and tried to sit up in his bed. Seeing his distress, Ma'ya rushed to his side. "Do not alarm thyself, my lord," she implored.

He took one deep breath after another until his heart stopped its pounding, until the harsh ringing in his ears ceased. He grew quiet, deep in thought.

"My dancing did not please thee," Ma'ya bemoaned, the golden tips of her breasts brushing against his chest as she bent over him.

"Thy dancing did please me," Seti assured her.

"Let me pleasure thee, my lord," Ma'ya said as she slid along his prone form like a sleek bronze snake.

But Seti demurred; his mind still racing. Who would be king once he became a "Westerner" and was buried in the great stone valley to the west of Thebes?

His firstborn son and heir was still young, head-strong, immature, and unfit to rule. With his death, Seti feared, the counselors would rule in his son's stead. The priests would gain even more power, their bureaucracy robbing his land of its vitality, its strength. His beloved Egypt, how could she survive without him?

He was born. He would soon die. Yet he would live again according to the *Book of the Dead*, which would be entombed between his legs. He must capture the power, the essence of himself—that of the last great king—while he still had the strength.

Seti knew the moment he had been waiting for was upon him. The time had come for the most sacred and secret of rituals. He held Ma'ya's arms firmly, for his own were suddenly endowed with superhuman strength. "I am thy king."

There was alarm in her dark eyes and he knew she heard the power in his voice. "Thou art my king," she repeated, her voice quavering.

His fingers dug into her flesh. "Thy god."

Her eyes dropped. "My god."

"Thou must obey thy king and god. Bring me a small glass jar from the table."

She blinked several times and repeated his words. "I will bring thee a small glass jar." She walked to the table and reached out for one of the beautiful, ornate gold containers.

"Not one of those," Seti said to her. "A plain one. An ordinary one will better suit my purpose."

Ma'ya chose a simple dark blue lapis lazuli container that was no more than four or five inches in height. She brought it to him.

"Thou hast chosen well," Seti said. Then he continued, mesmerizing her with his voice. "When the divine and powerful Merneptah Seti is brought to the Great Place prepared for him, thee, Ma'ya, royal cousin and consort, obedient and loving servant, must count this plain glass vessel among the many splendid treasures that will surround him as he enters the eternal afterlife. Hear and obey."

"I hear and obey," she said.

Seti sighed and lay back for a moment, releasing his grip on her. There was a spot or two of bright red blood on her flesh where his fingernails had cut her. Bruises were already forming where he had clasped her arm in a vow of life and death. "Go now and return only when the sun god Re has rowed his golden barge across the sky into the west. Allow no one to enter this room until that time. So I have said. So it must be done."

"So it must be done," Ma'ya repeated, picking up her linen dress and cloak and her soft leather slippers and leaving the palace room.

Once he was alone, Seti knew what he had to do. He picked up the small vial the priest-physician had placed on the table beside him and poured its contents into the uncorked glass jar. Then he took hold of himself and began to masturbate. As the moment of climax came upon him, he held up the lapis-colored vessel and with a shout that was exultant, triumphant, ejaculated the last of his precious seed into the waiting suppository. Then he began to recite in a powerful voice:

> Come Osiris, Horus, and Set,
> Come glorious Isis and her sister Nephthys, Anubis,
>   and Amon-Re,
> Hear me, Thoth, Ptah, Bes and Buto, Onouris and
>   Shu,
> I call upon thee, the mighty gods, to hear my
>   supplication,
> That the people will know the awful power of
>   Merneptah Seti,
> That his power will be the power of the gods,
> And the people will tremble in fear and make
>   offerings to appease the god whom they have
>   sorely offended.

With the closing words of his divine invocation—some might have called it a curse—Seti raised the small blue jar to his lips and drank deeply, reciting: "Birth. Death. Rebirth. Seed of his seed, I shall be reborn of Osiris, never to know death a second time." Then he uttered his secret name, that name known not even to his mother, and exhaled his spirit, his magic, all of his power into the glass receptacle.

He had only enough strength left to seal the jar with

a small wax plug and, clasping it firmly in his hand, let it fall to his side. With his final breath the great king said, "It is done."

It was evening. The sun god Re had quit the blue Egyptian sky to dwell with the Lord of Darkness for the twelve hours of the night.

It was time.

Ma'ya entered the palace room alone as she'd been instructed. She gracefully glided across the floor until she reached the bedside of the king. She saw that he was dead. Clasped in his hand was the small blue jar he had insisted she bring to him before leaving the room. Instinct guided her. She reached out and pried loose the jar from his lifeless fingers, invoking the protection of her patron goddess, Sekhmet-Bast-Re, she-with-the-head-of-a-male-and-the-body-of-a-woman-with-a-phallus.

Concealing the glass vessel in the folds of her robe, Ma'ya fell to her knees beside the pharaoh's gilded bed and cried out: "The king is dead! The king is dead!"

ONE

Las Vegas
The present day

Fear.

Adrian King could smell it. The stink of raw emotion filled his nostrils, burned the back of his throat, made his eyes see red; it flooded his senses and threatened to break through the protective shield that kept him in control, kept him sane. *Yet you draw closer to insanity, to madness, with each passing day,* Adrian reminded himself as his gaze swept the crowded casino.

The unmistakable odor of fear hit him again, harder this time, like a fist slamming into his gut. For a moment he was robbed of breath; he felt light-headed, dizzy. He swayed on his feet, then staggered back on his heels.

Adrian closed his eyes and inhaled deeply. He remembered a day many years before—*centuries before*—it was the time of his *hep-sed* celebration, the Festival of the Tail. How invincible he'd felt as he'd run the obstacle course that tested the physical prowess of the pharaoh, racing along the banks of the blue Nile, jumping high hurdles as if they were no more than a small hindrance in his way, wrestling the best of his personal guard and emerging victorious, shooting his arrows straight to their target.

He drew pleasure from the memory of the military campaigns he'd planned and successfully executed during the daylong battles he had fought as one of the Black Land's warrior-kings. He knew what his loyal troops had said of him more than three thousand years ago: Merneptah Seti, whose secret name was known not even to his mother, Horus incarnate, son of Amon-Re, the resurrected Osiris, King of Upper Egypt and Lower Egypt, Uniter of the Two Lands, descended of Tuthmosis, who had reigned nearly three hundred years before him, and of Merneptah and Seti, his namesakes, and even of the Great Ramses himself, was unequaled as a military commander and warrior.

Adrian called on that training and discipline now. He knew if he didn't take control of the situation it could quickly become dangerous, even life-threatening. Not to him, but to *them*: the people who were crammed into his casino three- and four-deep around the blackjack tables, the roulette wheels, even the slot machines.

For he could smell life, he could smell blood, he could *smell* emotions; especially primitive human emotions like anger and fear, hunger and thirst, greed and lust. It was these emotions that the throng of visitors brought with them to the Royal Palace Hotel and Casino night after night. To protect himself from the relentless assault on his senses, Adrian had learned to erect a barrier in his mind. Still, the stench and the temptation grew stronger with each passing day.

As did the hunger.

He took a moment to shore up his defenses before seeking out the source of the foul odor. It was a female, of that much he was certain. Women exuded fear differently than men.

With the instincts of a bird of prey he searched the area, zooming in for a moment on a cocktail waitress dressed in a skimpy costume. Like all those who served food and drink to his guests at the Royal Palace, she wore the traditional black wig of the ancient people. There was a golden collar plate around her throat and thick gold hoops dangling from her earlobes. Silver bracelets, inlaid with turquoise and carnelian and other semiprecious stones, adorned her wrists and ankles. Kohl outlined her eyes. Rouge colored her lips.

Only moments before, the waitress had dropped the drinks tray she'd been carrying, sending an assortment of crystal glasses, cocktail napkins embossed with an intertwining *R P,* and colorful straws flying in all directions. Wine, mixed drinks, and melting ice soaked into the lush carpet underfoot as the woman worked feverishly to clean up the mess before the floor manager noticed the accident.

Adrian put his nose a little higher in the air and sniffed again. She was afraid. Afraid of losing her job. Afraid for herself and for someone else, as well. A child. Afraid they would end up on the streets. Hungry. Homeless. Or worse. Still, this wasn't the smell that tormented him, repulsed him, *lured* him.

He quickly located another female: older, silver-haired, beautifully dressed and beautifully groomed. She was playing roulette. He noticed that her hands trembled as she counted and recounted the stack of chips in front of her. To one side, at her left elbow, was an empty glass. *Scotch whisky*. Her perfectly manicured fingernails scraped across the green felt table as she signaled a nearby cocktail waitress. She wanted—no, she *needed*—another drink.

The woman evoked an image in his mind of a faded, wasted rose, one that had lost its freshness and beauty and was now shriveled, dried, and brittle, the edges of its once-perfect petals withered and tinged with brown so dark as to be nearly black in color. *Funereal*. The pungent odor of decay clung to her skin, her clothing, even her perfectly coiffed hair. The woman was dying. And she was afraid of death.

Dying wasn't so bad, Adrian thought with a sardonic smile, if you didn't stay dead.

He remembered well the day of his own death. Limbs useless, muscles without strength, he had lain there helpless and motionless upon his bed. As with all the great profusion of furniture, jewelry, and riches he'd possessed, the bed had been the finest that Egyptian artisans could craft in his honor. The knobs of the slanted wood frame had been embossed with gold from the Nubian desert. The headrest and the footboard had been inscribed with the appropriate references to the god-king Merneptah Seti. The sides had been decorated with intricate inlays of ivory from Africa, silver from Syria, and lapis lazuli (blue had always been the favorite color of his people) from Badakshan. Along with his chairs and his cosmetic box, his jewelry and his best linen, the bed had been brought with him on that last pilgrimage up the Nile all the way from the capital city of Tell-el-Dab in the northern Delta.

Time had ceased to exist during that afternoon and evening as life had slowly slipped away from him, although he recalled performing the ancient rituals before exhaling his final breath.

He knew that his body had been secreted away to the Valley of the Kings, and what followed was an eternity of darkness. He could not have said how long he lay in his tomb, in his sarcophagus. Gradually he became aware that he was existing just below the level of consciousness. Little by little his senses heightened, intensified, grew acute, until he could smell life, until he could smell blood.

It was then he *awakened*.

For several years after returning to the living he read, studied, devoured information at an astounding rate. He taught himself history, religion, philosophy, economics, business, and languages. He chose a modern name: Adrian from the Old Latin, meaning "the Dark One," and "King," since he had always been a king—since that long-ago time when he was called Merneptah Seti, when he was the greatest ruler of the greatest desert land.

Now he resided in a different land, in a different desert. He had even traded one palace for another: His living quarters were the sumptuous penthouse atop the Royal Palace, where he had a panoramic view of the Las Vegas Strip and the Nevada desert beyond.

Adrian had realized right from the start what an asset

his special "abilities" were in a city like Las Vegas. He had been able to break into the tightly controlled circle of casino owners within a short period of time, thanks to his extraordinary powers and his immense personal wealth. Furthermore, the onslaught of emotions—the lifeblood of Sin City—had fed his need to feel alive again. He had vicariously experienced fear and rage and exhilaration and lust and desperation over and over again until what had once been a blessing had become a curse.

Now if he didn't keep his emotions under control, the hunger threatened to overpower him, to drive him to become what he feared most, what he abhorred above all else, what the ancients had called an Eater of Blood and a Breaker of Bones.

"Surely that path leads to madness and eternal damnation," Adrian said aloud as he stood in the crow's nest high above the casino and looked out over the blackjack tables and the roulette wheels, the slot machines and the craps tables, to the other end of the cavernous yet elegant room where the high rollers played baccarat and poker in semi-seclusion.

It was here that he took his place every night, dressed in an exquisitely tailored black tuxedo and a pristine white dress shirt of the finest Egyptian cotton, hair dark and, like Samson's in the Old Testament story, longer than was currently the fashion, eyes piercing, eyes that missed nothing, eyes that were the color of lapis.

Nearly thirty years ago when he'd arisen from his long slumber, Adrian had been surprised—stunned was not too strong a word—to gaze into one of the many ornate mirrors that had been buried with him and discover that his eyes had changed color as he slept. He realized it must have been the result of the lapis lazuli in the potion he had long ago ingested.

The stink of fear, awful fear, suddenly struck Adrian again. He scanned the casino until his gaze came to rest on a young creature on the opposite side of the Royal Palace from where he kept watch. He instantly knew her name: Candy. What kind of name was Candy for a full-grown female, even one with bleached blonde hair, and pretty, if common, features? he wondered.

"Candy" was tall and slender. Too slender for the disproportionately large size of her breasts. They were obviously fake, as so many were in this city of dreams and illusions. Mystified, Adrian shook his head and pondered, not for the first time, why so few in the modern world seemed happy with themselves. There was such unrest, such dissatisfaction, such a desperate desire to be someone else, anyone else, than who they were. These so-called civilized human beings wandered through life oblivious to the emotions roiling just beneath the surface. Emotions that could be the ruin of him, and the death of them.

The blonde was dressed in an expensive and revealing evening gown. Dangling from a gold chain around her throat was a sparkling gemstone the size of a plump, sweet fig. A ring on the middle finger of her right hand had a matching gemstone. Unlike her enhanced physical attributes, the stones were real. Once more Adrian shook his head with bemusement. In his time only the royal court and the wealthiest of his subjects could have afforded such luxury.

This is your time now, he admonished himself.

Candy was standing behind a young man named Jason, who was seated at a blackjack table; her hand was resting lightly on his shoulder. In front of Jason were at least a dozen stacks of chips in a rainbow of colors and denominations. He was winning. And winning big.

Adrian's attention reverted to the female. What was she afraid of? Was she afraid Jason would lose? Was she afraid he would win? That didn't make sense. Or perhaps she was afraid that he might be *discovered.*

Adrian nudged his mind closer to the action just as a roar went up from the crowd. Excitement rippled in the air. Electricity crackled around Jason as he miraculously beat the odds again. An enormous pile of chips was meted out by the dealer. His "guest" had won a princely sum.

Another emotion unexpectedly smashed into Adrian's chest, a gut-wrenching blow that nearly brought him to his knees. Through the sheer force of his will, trained and tempered in the heat of battle, he managed to stand his ground.

He shifted his focus to the one who was known as Jason. He immediately smelled avarice and ambition. He could see greed in the man's eyes. His pupils were dilated. His eyeballs were bulging. There were small beads of perspiration on his skin and dripping down the side of his face. His breathing was shallow and erratic. His heart was racing.

Adrian licked his lips. He could almost taste the young male's blood on his tongue.

Another hand or two were dealt and the stack of chips in front of the lucky player continued to grow at an alarming rate. Something didn't feel right. In fact, something felt very wrong. Adrian spoke into his head-piece. "Phelps?"

"Yes, Mister King," came the crisp response.

"Table forty-two. A man in a brown jacket with a tall, buxom blonde standing behind him."

Eric Phelps was immediately on the move. "I've never seen him before, Mister King. He's not one of our regulars." Phelps would know; he'd been Special Forces for a decade or two in the world's worse hell holes and had an uncanny memory for faces. "JDLR?"

Casino jargon for: *Just doesn't look right*. Adrian trusted his gut instincts; they had always served him well. "Yes. See if he's on our most-wanted list. And find out how much he's won."

Phelps reported back in less than five minutes. "His name is Jason Stanford-White, with a hyphen. He's not registered as a guest of the hotel. He arrived with the woman by taxi, not limo. He's been playing blackjack for the past two hours. He's drinking Chivas on the rocks. The blonde seems to favor apple martinis. And he's won close to seven hundred thousand."

"Card counter?"

"Or just very, very lucky, Mister King."

Adrian didn't believe in luck, either good or bad. Neither did Phelps. And although card counting wasn't illegal in the state of Nevada, he was well within his rights as a casino owner to have anyone suspected of the practice escorted off the premises and banned from ever returning. "Is he in the Griffin Book?"

"No, sir, he's not on the list of suspected cheats and

skilled gamblers, and there's no match in our database. But he could be new to Vegas."

Adrian could smell the man's—*the boy's*—smug satisfaction. He was cocky. He was gloating. And he was putting something over on the Royal Palace.

Nobody got the better of Adrian King.

Adrian touched the heavy gold signet ring on his finger: It was embedded with a scarab, symbol of resurrection, and a cartouche of ancient symbols that spelled out his name. He had always considered himself a just man: generous with those who earned his goodwill, and ruthless with those who deserved his wrath. This arrogant fool had no idea how easy he was getting off. In the past—the far distant past—a thief's hands would have been chopped off as punishment and as a warning to other transgressors who might presume to steal from their lord and master.

Adrian issued his orders. "Get Stanford-White's photograph for our files. Then escort him and the young lady from the casino."

"Yes, sir."

"And, Phelps, make certain they understand they won't be welcomed back to the Royal Palace."

Phelps snapped to attention. "I'll take care of it personally, Mister King. Consider it done."

At least that much hadn't changed. A word from him had once been enough to seal the fate of men and nations. *So it is said; so it must be done.* It held true today, although his empire was of a different kind and in a different country. He was well aware of what his employees said about him behind his back: that he had a nose for trouble, that he could foresee the future. They were closer to the truth than they realized. Adrian also knew that while they might trust him completely and implicitly, they considered him an enigma.

He trusted no one, with the exception of Rahotep. He confided in no one. He believed in no one but himself. And with good reason. As Merneptah Seti, as pharaoh, as god-king, he had experienced the ultimate betrayal—the betrayal of those closest to him, those who were sworn to serve him, those who professed to love him—and the memory was still fresh in his mind and heart even after all this time.

Adrian took a deep breath. The smell of fear had eased, subsided. The card counter was gone. Eric Phelps had done his job.

He took another deep breath and gazed out over the sea of sights and sounds and smells below him. Then they, too, faded until they were no more than white noise in the background. Emotions were his enemy, his Achilles heel, and they would be his downfall. He must stand guard against them every minute of every hour of every day. That was the price he paid for sanity.

For immortality.

I grow weary, he thought, and reached up to massage the side of his head where a residual pain had lodged in his brain. The time would soon come when he must choose: to walk into the desert, into the bright, eternal light where he would be consumed by the sun god Re, and his life would finally end, or surrender to the dark night where rage and hunger would overtake him, where he would be reduced to being no more than a feral animal that hunted and fed.

Adrian turned and reached for a glass of water on a

nearby table. Ice-cold water. Crystal clear water. Water in abundance. Water without end. This was true luxury. This was the one extravagance in the modern world that he savored and appreciated above all others. He raised the glass to his mouth. Then stopped.

He froze in place.

His nose went up in the air.

What was that scent?

He inhaled. It couldn't be. He must be mistaken. He inhaled again and held the fragrance in his lungs, allowed it to permeate his heart and mind and every cell of his body. He recognized the distinctive aroma of sandalwood and rare oils and precious herbs. It was a one-of-a-kind perfume of his own creation, one he had secretly concocted for a woman who had appeared to him long ago in his dreams. He hadn't smelled it in years. In centuries.

He must be wrong.

He was never wrong!

A love poem he had written eons before in her honor echoed through Adrian's mind:

> *Hail to thee, most mysterious and beauteous of*
> *   women,*
> *Consort of the god, beloved of him who wears the*
> *   two crowns,*
> *Thou art fair in face, graced with a body and a*
> *   spirit that is perfection.*
> *Isis incarnate, how the gods worship thee!*
> *Thy breasts art sweeter than honey,*
> *Thy beauty greater than the fabled Nefertiti,*
> *Thy skin finer than the gold of Kush.*

Thy eyes art the color of the sky at dusk,
Thy voice is more pleasing than the music of the
  harp, than the sound of the River of Life at dawn.
Thou art favored by the gods.
They call thee by name.
And when they see thee come it is said: The
  Beautiful One comes!

TWO

Christine Day couldn't believe her eyes. She stopped dead in her tracks, her weight evenly distributed on the heels of her sensible black pumps, and began to scrutinize the hieroglyphs carved into the great stone columns at the entrance to the hotel. She'd expected to see tacky. Not in the sense of cheap imitations—after all, it was widely known that Adrian King had spared no expense when he'd built the Royal Palace—but in the sense of fakes.

She reached out to touch the massive stone edifice in front of her, then jerked her hand back. Despite the seasonably warm weather, Christine was suddenly cold, chilled right down to the bone.

She was also wrong.

The hieroglyphs were real.

Real enough that she could read them, which is precisely what she did. The more she read, the more intrigued she became. She recognized the symbols. She quickly identified the name etched within the royal cartouche. She was familiar with the history recorded on the column: It was one of the bedtime stories that her grandfather had told her countless times when she was a little girl. It was about the heroic feats of Seti III, also known as Merneptah Seti, the warrior-king of the Nineteenth Dynasty and the last great pharaoh of ancient Egypt, the very pharaoh that her grandfather, and his grandfather before him, had spent a lifetime studying, researching, and digging for in the Valley of the Kings.

Life definitely had its ironies, she thought.

"Christine?" prompted an impatient male voice from the doorway to the hotel.

Even with a pair of dark sunglasses securely in place Christine had to shade her eyes against the setting sun as it reflected off the structures around her. She turned and discovered that her colleague was waiting for her. "Yes?"

"Are you coming? It's hotter than hell out here." It was Bryce St. Albans, and he was clearly in a hurry to get inside the Royal Palace and out of the heat.

Christine *almost* apologized for keeping him waiting until she remembered that Bryce had failed to show up that morning for her presentation on "DNA Testing: Establishing the Bloodline of the New Kingdom Pharaohs." It was considered a professional courtesy for scholars and researchers to attend each other's lectures, especially since she and Bryce were both on the staff of the University of Chicago, and had been selected by the Oriental Institute to attend this prestigious international conference.

And supposedly they were friends.

Five minutes . . . less than five minutes in the Nevada sun and her fellow Egyptologist was wilting like a hot-house flower. Christine wondered how Bryce, always fastidious from the top of his perfect blond head right down to his expensive designer loafers, managed the heat and the other "discomforts" of an onsite archaeo-logical dig. She didn't think she cared to find out.

"Why don't you go on without me," she urged him. "I know you want to have a drink and gamble a little. I think I'll take my time and look around. We'll meet up later."

"Suit yourself." Bryce St. Albans did an about-face and disappeared through the nearest set of doors.

Christine heaved a sigh of relief and walked up to the next towering stone column. This one, too, held an ac-count of the exploits of Merneptah Seti: It was a long and elaborate tale of how the pharaoh singlehandedly slew his enemies by the thousands in battle, emerging unscathed and victorious, how he caused the Nile to spill over its banks every year, insuring the richness of the soil, the abundance of the crops, and the prosperity of his people, how he was both king and god, and how he was able to defy even death itself.

She read the final inscription in a reverent whisper. " 'Raise yourself. You have not died. Your life force will dwell with you always. You are among the living in this land forever.' "

Again, Christine shivered and wrapped her arms

around herself. Silly to feel chilled when it was still at least ninety degrees outside and she was wearing one of her standard uniforms: a tailored gray suit with a lighter-shade gray blouse underneath, its severe neckline softened by a silk scarf.

Silly, perhaps, but words had power. Incredible power. That's what the Egyptians had believed millennia ago. That's what she believed herself. Besides, she'd always had this connection with ancient Egypt for as long as she could remember. Even as a child she'd had an uncanny (although her family preferred the word *precocious*) ability to read and understand hieroglyphs.

Christine decided it was time to move inside since a thorough study of the columns would take hours, perhaps even days. As she approached the hotel entrance a doorman suddenly appeared. "Welcome to the Royal Palace, ma'am."

When had she become "ma'am" instead of "miss"? *When you hit the Big 3-0*, she told herself, and that was several years ago. "Thank you," Christine said politely and entered the lobby.

It was surprisingly quiet. There were thick, lush carpets underfoot and painted ceilings high overhead. The furniture appeared to be crafted from the finest imported woods and was artfully arranged in conversation groups. There were huge earthenware pots filled with papyrus and other exotic plants, and living palm trees that soared toward the sky depicted above in elaborate detail. The air was cool, not cold, and subtly perfumed with a hint of spice, perhaps cinnamon.

Christine paused for a moment in front of a pair of

seated stone statues. There was a discreet plaque at the base that read: KING MERNEPTAH SETI AND HIS CHIEF QUEEN, NEFERTARI, CIRCA 1198 B.C.E. (ORIGINAL IN THE LOUVRE).

The statues were beautiful. Breathtaking. Only an expert would have guessed they were reproductions. *That and the fact the originals were on display thousands of miles away in Paris*, Christine thought, smiling to herself. Adrian King must have hired only the best artisans, stonemasons, and sculptors.

She approached the first of several document cabinets and peered down at the single sheet of papyrus encased within its protective glass. It was a list of funereal objects and was written in a beautiful and ancient hand. She scanned down the page until she came to the last entry. She read it once, twice, then a third time.

Christine stood there for a moment. A thrill surged through her. The final item on the page read: *THE RECIPE FOR A PERFUMED OIL CREATED BY THE KING*; then the word *MISSING*.

Missing no longer, she thought.

From there she wandered on to another display and then another, paying little attention to where she was going. Her entire focus was on the collection of splendid artifacts and expertly crafted reproductions she discovered at every turn.

Around the next corner was a promenade with human-headed sphinxes lining either side; they were reminiscent of the avenue of great stone sphinxes lining the processional ways or *dromoi* leading to the temple of Luxor.

Continuing her explorations, Christine found herself in a hallway with an exquisite mosaic embedded in the floor. The small, brightly colored tiles depicted the Osiris legend: the ancient story of betrayal, murder, and resurrection.

According to Egyptian myth, Osiris was killed and then dismembered by his evil brother Seth, who scattered his body parts throughout the Black Land. Osiris's wife, Isis, was able to recover and reconstitute his body, except for his genitalia, which had been consumed by the Nile carp and other fish of the River of Life. An artificial phallus had to be created in place of a flesh and blood one, so that Osiris might be deemed whole again. It was then Osiris became the first mummy and was able to take his rightful place among the gods.

"Osiris, who is eternally good and incorruptible, who is chief of the Westerners, who is ruler of the underworld and judge of the dead, and with whom Isis conceived the child Horus, ruler of the living and avenger of his father's murder," Christine read aloud from the hieroglyphs incorporated into the design.

She finally looked up and realized that she was alone at the end of a deserted corridor, standing transfixed in front of a pool of water. She found herself entranced by the sound of a crystalline fountain as it emptied into the pool, and the heavy, exotic scent of flowers carried by a faint breeze that stirred the living lotus plants.

Lilies floated on top of the water creating a sense of serenity and tranquility. She dipped her fingertips into the pool and skimmed them along its surface, and suddenly she was immersed in a flood of feelings, feelings of déjà-vu, and she had one of her "waking" dreams.

She was in a lush and ancient garden. The sun god Re loomed on the horizon; the sky was painted with the deepest and purest shades of pink and purple and azure. It was evening. There was a man present. He was sitting on a stone bench beside a courtyard pool. She was bathing in its dark blue waters. The lotus leaves seemed to uphold her nude body as she floated among them. A vine caught on her leg and was then dragged across the tender flesh between her thighs. The air was warm and the water was warm, and yet when her bare breasts broke the surface of the pool, she felt a chill and her nipples hardened into small morsels of fruits, tender fruits, sweet fruits.

She smiled up at the man invitingly. He rose from the bench, dropped the simple loincloth he wore, and waded into the water. Once he was standing in the waist-deep pool, he pulled her toward him. His eyes—she couldn't discern their color—suddenly changed, grew darker, hotter.

His hands covered her breasts. He caressed them, gently at first, until she moaned, "Harder." He caught her nipple between his thumb and forefinger and squeezed, and the breath caught in her throat. Then his fingers were replaced with his teeth and his tongue, and sensations washed over her like a small tidal wave.

She opened her eyes and studied the contrast of his dark hair against her pale skin, skin that was luminous in the evening light. She watched, mesmerized, as he took her between his lips and sucked her into his mouth. She felt her nipple harden on the tip of his tongue and she couldn't stop another moan of pure erotic pleasure.

Then both of their mouths were open; tongues were intertwined, sliding in and out between moist lips. She must have him. She knew she wouldn't be satisfied until they were naked, flesh against flesh, and demanding release from the exquisite torture.

Beads of perspiration gathered above her lips, in the shadows between her breasts and farther down, at the sensitive and intimate juncture of her thighs. His skin was covered with a musk-scented sweat that drew her in as if they were wild animals and it was mating season. His body was hard and muscular.

Hot flesh was pressed to even hotter flesh. He slipped a finger into her, then two, stealing her breath away. She reached for him, measured him, stroked him. Her fingers feathered across his mouth, his tongue, his throat, down his neck, across his chest and ribs, along his abdomen, dipping below the water, below his waist, brushing over a tangle of masculine hair until she clasped him in her hand. She squeezed the hard, smooth length of him, and he drew in a breath.

She lay back in the warm water and opened her legs. He came to her and raised her hips up out of the pool. He surged forward. He tasted her on his lips. He licked her. He took small, sensual nips. He savored the feel, the smell, the texture of her. He thrust his tongue deep inside of her. Her body throbbed.

Then the man pulled her toward him and speared her with his flesh. He took her again and again in the ritual "water dance." It was an exquisitely, tortuously slow dance. She cried out, grabbed at his shoulders, sunk her nails into him. Her heat rose up to burn him. Her excitement excited him.

He thrust harder and harder, deeper and deeper, over and over again. Muscles strained to the limit. Hearts pounding wildly. Hips thrashing fast and furious. Then with a shout, he emptied himself into the willing vessel of her body, and when he was finally finished, he lay back in the water and floated beside her.

It was then Christine awakened.

She was still standing in front of the clear pool of water in the Royal Palace. Her heart was beating wildly in her chest. Her clothes were damp. Her silk blouse was clinging to her skin. Her sunglasses were slipping down the bridge of her nose. There was a fine sheen of perspiration on her upper lip. She got a tissue from her handbag—she was actually shaking—and blotted her mouth.

Even without a mirror she knew her face was flushed. Her legs were quivering and threatened not to support her weight. She'd worn her hair up today in a French twist, but now there were tendrils trailing along her nape and around her ears.

What had come over her?

What in the world had she been thinking?

She *hadn't* been thinking. For a little while, although she honestly couldn't have said how long she'd been standing there, she had been a creature of pure emotion, lost in a world of senses and sensations.

Stuffing the damp tissue back into her handbag, Christine reached up to tidy her hair and discovered her hands were trembling. This was ridiculous. She was a woman who prided herself on her self-control. Sexual fantasies, especially explicit sexual fantasies, weren't her style.

She had barely regained her composure when she heard the distinctive click of shoes on the tile floor behind her. Christine turned, then inhaled sharply.

She was standing face to face with the man she had just seen in her erotic dream.

THREE

Adrian allowed the sweet scent to wash over him, to bathe his senses in its exotic and sensual perfume. A perfume he remembered well. A perfume he had created for a woman who had first appeared in his dreams more than thirty centuries ago.

How could the female standing in front of him here, now, so many thousands of years later, smell of this one-of-a-kind fragrance?

He tilted his head to one side and, with eyes closed and nostrils flaring, breathed in again, filling his lungs with the scent of the ancient oil as it emanated from the woman's skin, from the tiny pulse points on the underside of her wrists, where he could clearly see rivulets of blue through the transparency of her flesh (how like the Blue Nile her veins appeared!) and just there at the base of her pale throat where he could mark the beats of her heart, hear its rhythmic cadence as surely as if it resided within his own breast, smell the lifeblood, metallic, iron-rich, coppery, as it coursed through her body, and there where silky wisps of fine gossamer hair caressed her nape.

He opened himself up and allowed the odor to be infused into his bloodstream down to the smallest capillary, to permeate every cell of bone and muscle, and finally to flow unimpeded into his heart and mind. He was determined to know what the woman was thinking, what she was feeling. An easy enough thing to do with these humans.

Aren't you human? Adrian paused and contemplated his own question for a moment, twisting his mouth into a semblance of a smile—or perhaps it was more of a predatory grin.

He was human on some level, he supposed, but as Merneptah Seti he had been raised as a warrior, as a prince, as the rightful heir to the throne of the Black Land. As pharaoh he had been venerated by his people, believed by them to be both mortal and divine, worshiped as half-man, half-god. It was he who imposed order and prevented chaos. It was he who preserved and, if necessary, restored harmony to the universe. Power was addictive, and he had been all-powerful. Heady stuff for a mere mortal.

If, indeed, he had ever been mortal.

Since his awakening Adrian had also discovered that his sense of smell, his eyesight, even his hearing had become so acute, a whole world had opened to him that had previously been known only to the wolf, the eagle, and the most cunning hunters of the forest and the desert. A world where even the slightest movement—no more than a mere whisper of a creature's breath or a solitary flutter of a terrified heart—could deliver prey into the lightning-quick death grip of a hunter's jaws.

Adrian took in another deep inhalation, simultaneously dreading and anticipating the flood of emotions that would rush into him, fill him, propel him inextricably closer to that point of no return. But there was only the odor of the ancient oil.

Nothing more.

Nothing less.

He was stunned. This was unheard of. It was without precedence. It confounded him. Perplexed him. *Intrigued* him. He took a step nearer, nudging the woman standing in front of him with his mind. Still, nothing. Then he pushed harder, but it was as though he had run headlong into a solid brick wall.

By all the demons of the underworld, by the devourer of unrighteous hearts and the discontented dead, this woman, this creature, seemed to be able to prevent him from reading her thoughts!

He had never encountered a human being with this ability before. Usually he had to stand guard against the outpouring of emotions, protect himself from the deluge that was unleashed like a dam bursting its concrete and steel barriers.

How could this insignificant female, hair and clothing dishabille, sunglasses hiding her eyes, how could she stop him from smelling, from seeing, from *knowing*?

For a moment Adrian was tempted to command her to remove the offending glasses and explain herself.

Who are you? That's what he really wanted to know. *And why are you wearing the perfume that I created for the Beautiful One who visited me in my dreams?*

Adrian opened his eyes and consciously relaxed his shoulders. He widened his stance by six or seven inches to put himself and his "guest" at ease. Using every modicum of the self-control (for surely self-control was the true measure of a great warrior or a great king, or even of a god) he inquired, "Are you lost?"

"No," the woman replied. A moment later she appeared to change her mind. She raised her arms and then let them fall to her sides again. "Well, yes, I suppose I am. I was so intent on looking at your exhibits and studying the hieroglyphic inscriptions that I didn't pay any attention to where I going."

"And you ended up here?"

She nodded. "I ended up here."

Adrian suddenly found himself amused. The unflattering and rather severe business suit the young woman wore was at such odds with the wild flush on her cheeks, with the damp tendrils of hair that had escaped the French twist secured with pins at the nape of her neck, with the telltale odor of sex that clung to her from head to toe.

"Perhaps if you . . ." Adrian gestured, indicating the sunglasses she was wearing.

"Oh, of course." She reached up and removed the pair of dark glasses and stuffed them into her handbag. She put her shoulders back and lifted her head.

That was better. Much better.

For the first time he could see her eyes: They were

intelligent, but wary, guarded, distrustful. They were eyes that concealed far more than they revealed.

If the poets were right, if the eyes were the windows to the soul, then this woman was going to present a worthy challenge, Adrian thought as he took a step closer to his quarry.

FOUR

His eyes were blue.

Christine hadn't expected that. She'd just assumed they would be brown. Dark brown, in fact. An illogical conclusion to have jumped to, she realized, since she had never met the man.

Well, yes and no.

Only moments ago he had been making love to her in her "waking" dream, and she swore she could still taste him on her lips, smell him on her skin, feel him move inside of her. No wonder she was disconcerted. And a little embarrassed.

She knew who he was, of course. She'd caught an occasional glimpse of him in newspapers and magazines, although she had to admit those photographs had not done him justice.

The man was Adrian King: multimillionaire—

billionaire, some speculated—although no one seemed to know for certain how much wealth he'd managed to accumulate since he had arrived on the scene, taking Las Vegas by storm.

Casino owner, real estate magnate, philanthropist, patron of the arts, a gentleman with exceptional taste (it was said that he possessed one of the best private collections of Egyptian antiquities in the world as well as one of the best wine cellars), Adrian King was a man with the Midas touch, a man of many talents, a man of mystery, and, in the end, a man of dubious lineage.

There were rumors that he was a nobody and came from nowhere. There were an equal number of rumors that his blood was blue, that he was of royal birth, that he could trace his family tree back to princes, even to kings, although exactly what country or potentate was a further source of speculation.

Whatever his background Adrian King exuded power as if it were his birthright, as if it had permeated his heart and mind and soul, even his skin, for thousands of years.

Christine took an involuntary step toward him. There was something about Adrian King that drew her in, mesmerized her without a word, with only a glance.

It was his eyes, she decided. It took all the willpower she possessed to look away from those eyes, eyes that burned like that dichotomy of hot and cold blue fire buried deep in the heart of the rarest and bluest of blue sapphires.

The man standing in front of her was tall, but not exceptionally so. She estimated he was six feet in height, give or take an inch either way. His shoulders were broad and his body was muscular. His tuxedo jacket had been custom tailored to his physique and yet there was a suggestion of muscles straining beneath the expensive material.

The word *warrior* popped into Christine's head, and she remembered another time when that description had been applied to a man, a very special man.

"The king was a warrior in those days," her grandfather told Christine as he sat in a chair by her bedside and regaled her with stories of ancient Kemet.

She was nearly nine years old, all arms and legs, and *ears* whenever her grandfather returned home from one of his extended trips to Egypt and paid her a visit. "Tell me more," she pleaded.

Lawrence Day was a born storyteller, and Christine was a willing and captive audience, which suited them both. "The king was omnipotent. He was believed to be part god, part man; a ruler of great intellectual and physical strength; a true leader. He rode into battle at the front of his troops, inspiring them by his example." Grandfather's voice rang out with admiration and with something more, something magical, and a shiver ran down her spine.

"Have you ever seen one of these kings?" Christine wanted to know, leaning closer.

"Oh, yes," her grandfather said in an awed whisper, and her heart began to beat a little faster.

She must know. "When?"

"I was only a year or two older than you are when my parents gave their permission for me to travel to Egypt with my grandfather on one of his digs."

Christine wished she would be allowed to travel with Grandpapa to see the Pyramids at Giza and the Valley of the Kings, but she may as well have wished for the moon. Her parents didn't approve of her fascination with ancient Egypt; they never had, they never would.

Her grandfather continued his story. "That trip happened to coincide with the discovery of the tomb of Tutankhamen in the Valley of the Kings." There was a brief pause. "Little did I realize then that Howard Carter's crowning moment was also going to become the defining moment of my life." Lawrence Day stopped and stared off into space. Christine dared not interrupt whatever thoughts or memories were flowing through his mind. Eventually her grandfather came back to the present, as he always did, and said in a matter-of-fact manner, "Of course, Tutankhamen was still a boy—well, according to most Egyptologists a young man of no more than sixteen or seventeen—when he died."

And a minor king, Christine thought, despite the riches found in his tomb. "Do you believe in the curse of Tutankhamen?" She was intrigued by the idea of curses.

"No," he said, rubbing his hand back and forth across his moustache in a typically masculine gesture. "Modern scholars seem to agree that the deaths following the discovery of Tutankhamen's tomb were either coincidence or unfortunate accidents or possibly the result of exposure to an ancient and lethal strain of bacteria that was released when the burial chamber was opened."

Desecrated, Christine thought. But she did not say

the word out loud. Nor did she confide to her grandfather that she believed in curses. But she most certainly did!

She stuffed another feather pillow behind her back and sat up straighter in bed. "What of the great warrior-kings who came after Tutankhamen?"

"There is one especially I would like to have seen for myself," her grandfather said with a regret that had been a part of him for as long as she could remember.

"You haven't found your warrior-king?"

"No. I haven't found the one I seek. The same one my grandfather spent his life searching for."

"I know which king you mean," she said solemnly. "Seti the Third, also known as Merneptah Seti."

"That's right." Lawrence Day patted her head. "You're a very bright child."

Christine wanted to say: *"Sometimes I don't feel like a child, Grandpapa. I have dreams. Strange and wonderful dreams."* But something held her back. She was already aware that she was "different," that she was an eccentric in a family of eccentrics.

Then her grandfather inquired, "How is your study of hieroglyphs going?"

"I'm getting better at reading them," she replied, trying not to sound as though she were bragging. In truth, she not only read years beyond her age in English and French, but she was fluent in ancient Egyptian: both forms of the written language, hieroglyphs and hieratic, and the spoken language. But she sensed it was also best to keep this information to herself.

Lawrence Day reached into his coat pocket and took out a piece of papyrus. He handed it to her. Christine carefully unrolled the piece of paper and quickly read the list of symbols. It was a recipe, but a very special kind of recipe.

"What's this?" she asked, although she already knew the answer to her own question.

Her grandfather was watching her closely. "You know what it is, don't you?"

Christine couldn't lie to him. She looked up and gray eyes—eyes the color of the sky as evening fell upon the ancient land—stared back at her, eyes that reflected the color and intensity and intelligence of her own. "Yes, Grandpapa," she said in a whisper.

He bit back a smile. "What is it, Christine?"

She moistened her lips before answering. "It's a recipe for a scented oil."

"Who is it written by?"

She didn't have to glance down at the papyrus, for she already knew the answer to that question as well. "King Merneptah Seti."

"And who has he created this perfumed oil for?"

"The woman who visits him in his dreams. The woman he calls 'his secret.'"

"What do you think that means?" Grandpapa's question surprised her, for he was speaking to her as if he'd forgotten for a moment that she was nine years old. Well, she would be nine in another two months and thirteen days.

"Normally a king would have his dreams interpreted by his priests, but Seti decided to keep this dream a secret from them, from everyone." Christine gave her head an emphatic shake and stared at the papyrus through the pair of thick glasses that were settled on her child's nose. "I think the pharaoh was in love with the woman who came to him in his dreams."

Her grandfather laughed; it was not an unkind laugh, for her grandfather was not an unkind man. "What would a child know of such love?"

She couldn't explain it to herself, let alone to him. It wasn't as if she understood the intimate details of love between a man and a woman, but she understood longing, she understood loneliness; she understood something that she couldn't put into words.

She also couldn't explain how she knew what the perfumed oil smelled like but she did, as surely as if she were inhaling it at that very moment.

Christine blinked owlishly and added, "It must have been very lonely to be a king."

"Yes, I suppose it was," Lawrence Day agreed, stroking his moustache again. Then he leaned back in the overstuffed chair and let out a long sigh. "I am getting old, Christine. Time is running out for me."

"No," she protested, the sudden sting of tears burning the back of her throat. She could not bear the thought of losing the one person who shared her passion for ancient Kemet, the one person who might understand what her dreams meant.

Her grandfather's eyes closed for a moment. "I fear I will never find Seti now."

That's when she made him a promise. "One day I'll find your king for you, Grandfather," she said with a conviction that wasn't in the least childlike.

Lawrence Day opened his eyes, and with a melancholy smile said, "Perhaps you will."

It was an hour or two before Christine finally fell asleep, the scent of the ancient oil filling her senses, filling her dreams, as surely as if it had permeated her skin—and her heart and soul.

Christine came back to the present to find herself still staring at Adrian King.

His hair was dark, black actually, the shade of black that almost had a blue sheen to it, which made his eyes appear all the bluer. It was slightly wavy and brushed the collar of his elegant tuxedo jacket, and when he moved his head she caught a glimpse of gold and realized he must be wearing earrings.

That surprised her. Most of the men who sported earrings these days were athletes, and they usually wore large diamond studs. *Bling*. Not that she considered herself to be on the cutting edge when it came to designer jewelry or clothes. She knew more about the styles worn three thousand years ago than she did the latest fashion trends.

Christine opened her mouth to say something about the impressive collection on display at the Royal Palace when Adrian King took two steps toward her and stopped.

He frowned, then narrowed his blue eyes and demanded to know, "Who are you?"

FIVE

"I'm Doctor Christine Day," the young woman said, looking Adrian right in the eye. She was wearing a pair of high heels, which made her nearly as tall as him so it was a relatively easy thing for her to do. But that wasn't what impressed Adrian. What impressed him was the fact she seemed undaunted.

Christine Day was either very courageous or very foolish, he thought. Without exception humans were intimidated by him—male and female. Yet this woman didn't appear to be the least bit afraid. He wondered if she knew who he was.

Adrian arched a quizzical brow. "Exactly what kind of doctor, are you, *Doctor* Christine Day?"

"I have a Ph.D. in Egyptology," she said, returning his gaze unflinchingly.

Irony. That was the only word for it. Here was a

modern woman bathed in the ancient scent, and it turned out that she was an expert on Kemet, on the Black Land, on *his* land.

Perhaps there was more Ms. Day would offer if he waited. He could afford to wait. After all, he had all the time in the world.

"I have a second degree in archaeology," she volunteered. He was patient; he remained silent. The only sound in the deserted corridor was the fountain flowing into the lotus-filled pool behind them. "And another in ancient history."

Adrian slipped one hand into the pocket of his tuxedo jacket. "Ancient history?"

"Specifically the time period from 1500 to 1000 B.C.E."

It might be ancient history to her, but it seemed like only yesterday to him, Adrian thought with a sardonic smile. Still, his interest was piqued. In fact, he hadn't been this curious about anything or anyone in a very long time.

"You've apparently spent a great deal of your life in the pursuit of knowledge," he said.

His guest tilted her head to one side, exposing the long, slender column of her neck. Her skin was like fine porcelain, her veins like faint cracks beneath its surface. There was only the merest suggestion of a pulse just there below her ear and there in the small indentation at the base of her throat.

"I've been an avid reader for as long as I can remember," she said, reaching up to tuck an errant strand of chestnut-brown hair behind one ear. "I believe that knowledge—learning, if you will—is a lifelong pursuit."

Tearing his eyes away from that nearly impercepti-
ble and yet hypnotic heartbeat buried underneath the
soft, alabaster flesh, Adrian said, "As do I."

He believed in the pursuit of knowledge as surely as
he believed that living forever was his birthright as
king, as pharaoh, as a god, especially one whose existence had been cut short through no fault of his own, but
by the treachery of others. As an immortal being he was
entitled to all the time he wanted, needed, desired, in order to study, to travel, to collect beautiful objects, to savor the best that life had to offer.

But Adrian had discovered that every blessing came
with its own damning curse, that there was a price to be
exacted for the privilege of eternal existence.

Sometimes it seemed like his life stretched out in front
of him like the sands of the Sahara; he traversed one dune
only to behold another identical dune in front of him, then
another and another and another. Neverending. Endless.
Always the same, and yet constantly shifting underfoot.

He was also aware that the hunger was beckoning to
him, tempting him, seducing him, luring him into cross-
ing that line and becoming a true creature of the night.
In the past several months he had come to understand
that there was a fate worse than death, that life without
end, life spent as a monster, as an Eater of Blood and a
Breaker of Bones, was really no life at all.

In fact, the prospect of such a life was depressing.

By all the demons of the Underworld and the Swal-
lower of the Dead, he was starting to sound like these
feeble-minded human beings who did nothing but talk
about their feelings and who excused every shortcom-
ing by labeling it an emotional problem!

Adrian abruptly changed the subject and said to his guest, "What are you doing in Las Vegas?"

"I'm attending a conference of renowned Egyptologists at the university," she said, and he suspected that was a hint of a smile at the corners of Christine Day's mouth.

His brows climbed. "Are you a renowned Egyptologist?"

A slight crease formed between the woman's eyes. "I have a certain reputation," was her guarded response.

Adrian made a motion with his other hand and realized he was waving his cartouche ring in her face. "And what would that reputation be, Doctor Day?"

She did not immediately answer him. Instead, she said, "Egyptology is part science, part art, and part intuition. It's also a very competitive field. In addition to an undergraduate degree in art history, anthropology or classical studies, or a similar discipline, it requires years of specialized graduate study. Since so much of the research that has been done is written in German and French, anyone aspiring to be an Egyptologist must also study those languages."

Adrian gave her a speculative glance and said, "*Sprechen Sie Deutsch?*"

"*Ja.*"

"*Parlez-vous français?*"

"*Oui. Et vous?*" she countered.

Adrian nodded. "I travel extensively, and I have business interests in a number of countries. It seemed judicious to learn to speak their languages."

Besides, a man didn't acquire enormous wealth or attain the highest level of society in the world, ancient or modern, without knowing what most people did not know. Long ago, during his reign as Merneptah Seti, only a small percentage of his subjects had been able to read or write. Even so, as pharaoh, he had made certain that he knew more than anyone else in his kingdom. That still held true today, in this modern kingdom he had created for himself.

Adrian suddenly realized he couldn't remember the last time he had held a real conversation with someone. Since his awakening he had been able to ascertain what these mortals were thinking and feeling before they uttered a word.

Not so with Christine Day. Conversing with her was a unique experience. It was also hard work. There were no shortcuts. He had none of the usual advantages. He would actually have to concentrate, to listen, to read between the lines, to observe her body language. If he wanted answers, he'd have to go about getting them the old-fashioned way: by asking her questions.

In the end, it would be worth the effort, Adrian reminded himself. He must find out why she smelled of the ancient oil.

He paused and passed his tongue along the sharp, serrated edges of his teeth. He tasted blood; his own blood. He wiped the back of his hand across his mouth; it came away clean. He swallowed the drops of metallic elixir, savoring their flavor for a moment, then turned his attention to the woman standing in front of him. "When did you first become interested in Egyptology?"

"It's always been my passion," she said, and reached up to straighten the silk scarf around her neck; it was a brilliant shade of scarlet and the only splash of color against an otherwise ordinary gray blouse and an equally ordinary and nondescript gray business suit.

Always meant different things to different people, of course. For Christine Day, who appeared to be in her late twenties or early thirties, it no doubt translated into the last ten or fifteen years. For an older human being, it might mean decades. But for him, *always* was counted in centuries, even in millennia.

"Always?" Adrian repeated.

She tempered her response. "Ever since I was a child of three or four."

Her answer surprised him. "So young?"

His guest cast her eyes downward for a moment and appeared to be studying the mosaic under their feet: It was, appropriately, the Osiris legend. When artisans were working in this section of the Royal Palace, he had been adamant about the placement of the exquisite tiles and the story they would tell. It was a story that he kept close to his heart so he would never forget.

The young woman moistened her lips before finally saying, "I've always had an intuitive grasp of what life must have been like in ancient Egypt."

There was that word again: *always*.

Adrian saw her struggle to explain. "I can't explain it," she told him. "It's simply been true for as long as I can remember."

He was curious. "Is that the reason for the reputation you mentioned?"

She nodded her head and admitted, "I know things that I really shouldn't know."

Intriguing. "Education alone never guarantees understanding, of course," he said. Then he suggested,

"Perhaps your grasp of the ancient world is where your intuition enters into the picture."

She looked up at him. "Perhaps."

Adrian closed his eyes and took a deep breath. He held the scent of the one-of-a-kind oil in his lungs. Then he opened his eyes and exhaled slowly. "Your perfume is lovely."

She blinked. "Thank you."

"And most unusual. I don't believe I've ever smelled a fragrance quite like it."

Her chin rose a fraction. "I made it myself."

That wasn't the answer he was expecting. Or seeking.

"It's based on an ancient recipe," she said.

Adrian went still as stone.

There was a short silence. "The recipe was written on a piece of papyrus my grandfather gave me when I was a child. I was only nine years old at the time." Ms. Day paused, then said in a whisper, "I consider it my most cherished possession."

Adrian clenched a fist at his side. "How did your grandfather come by this piece of papyrus?"

"His grandfather gave it to him. The story goes that when my great-great-grandfather was a young man of no more than twenty or twenty-one he went on his first expedition to Egypt. He called it beginner's luck when he stumbled across the ancient papyrus and a cache of other artifacts hidden in a cave in the Valley of the Kings."

"When was this?

She thought for moment. "Before the turn of the last century. I believe the year was 1875."

"What was your great-great-grandfather doing in the Valley of the Kings?" he asked, a bit too quickly.

"He was searching for the tomb of King Merneptah Seti, Seti the Third." She watched him with an unreadable expression on her face. "As a matter of fact, the same pharaoh who is described in detail on the columns of your hotel and who is on display in your front lobby."

The hair stood on end at the back of Adrian's neck. Could it be mere coincidence a young woman showed up at his hotel tonight, smelling of the ancient oil, and she turned out to be from a family who were experts on *him*? He wasn't sure he believed in coincidences.

"So, you see, the papyrus has been handed down from one generation of Egyptologists to the next. My grandfather and his grandfather are gone now, so I am its keeper." The scarf slipped off Christine Day's shoulders and floated to the floor in a pile of scarlet silk. For a moment it looked like a pool of blood.

"Allow me," Adrian said, as he had bent over and retrieved the scarf for her.

"Thank you," she said, stashing the silky material in her handbag.

"You're welcome," he replied, with the merest bow of his head, only enough to be polite, certainly not as a gesture of obeisance. By all the gods, he was still too much of a king in his heart and soul to show deference to anyone.

"The strange thing is," his guest continued, "from the moment I first read the papyrus as a child I knew what the scented oil would smell like. It was as if it had been created for me." Then Christine Day looked up at him and smiled.

And with that smile she was—transformed.

Adrian felt a shock of recognition slam through him.

His heart began to pound in his chest, hard and fast and furious. It crashed against his ribs like a fierce storm buffeting a ragged and rocky coastline. It threatened to crush his bones, to rip his muscles to shreds, to tear through his flesh and spill his life essence in a torrent of red. His emotions welled up, swamping him, engulfing him, drowning out his awareness of everything and everyone else.

How could he have been so blind?

He *knew* that smile.

He *knew* that face.

This was the woman who haunted his dreams.

He thought of the closing lines of the love poem he had written for her: *Thou art favored by the gods. They call thee by name. And when they see thee come it is said: The Beautiful One comes!*

SIX

Adrian King was staring at her as if he had seen a ghost. His eyes suddenly darkened to the color of a midnight sky. His features were drawn, delineated, gaunt. The blood drained from his face. Christine thought she saw him sway on his feet. Concerned, she took a step toward him. "Are you all right?"

The man didn't speak. He simply held up his hand commanding her to stop where she was.

Christine froze in place. A moment or two passed before she realized that her host was muttering under his breath. It took another few seconds before it registered that the language he was speaking wasn't English, but the language of the ancient Egyptians.

His accent was unlike any she had ever heard. She listened carefully but she couldn't make out his exact words. She finally decided to try a formal greeting in the same tongue: *"May nothing evil have power over you; may the eye of Horus be your protection; may the gods smile upon you."*

Adrian King responded in kind: *"May crocodiles not consume you; may your heart be pure and lighter than the feather of Maat; may the Great Eye watch over you."*

"I should have known you'd be fluent in the ancient language, Mister King," she said in English.

He appeared to recover his composure. "You know who I am then," he said.

"Yes, I do." There were few people in this town who wouldn't know who he was.

"Still, I'm remiss. I should have introduced myself earlier." He reached out and took her hand in his. His touch was both hot and cold, heating her blood even as a shiver of icy awareness trickled down her spine. "I am Adrian King," he said.

It was Christine's turn to be confounded. Her mind went blank. She couldn't seem to form a single coherent thought. She was pretty sure that she had already told him her name, but she gave it again, anyway. "I'm Christine Day."

"*Doctor* Christine Day," he quickly corrected, and she felt herself redden.

She supposed she had made a point of using her professional title. And why not? She had worked long and hard for her academic degrees, always striving to be first in her class, to be the best of the best, so no one could say to her face (or behind her back, for that matter) that her success had anything to do with her grandfather or with his grandfather before him.

While she respected the memory and the reputations of both men—Lawrence and Clarence Day had, after all, been highly regarded scholars and renowned Egyptologists in their time—she wanted her success to be . . . well, *hers*.

This is your time now, Christine, she reminded herself.

In any event, she had encountered skepticism before when it came to her particular talents, beginning with her own parents, then her teachers and professors, and currently a number of colleagues, including Bryce St. Albans.

Christine straightened her suit jacket and squared her shoulders. "You have a very impressive collection, Mister King."

"Then you must allow me to show you around the Royal Palace, Doctor Day." His offer was unexpected. "You are one of the few people who can truly appreciate what I've achieved here."

She hesitated. "Well . . ."

"I would like to very much, Christine," he said smoothly, and yet in a voice that would brook no argument. Then he added, "You will address me as Adrian."

Her first inclination was to refuse. She didn't like being ordered about by anyone, and Adrian King's "offer" had sounded very much like an order. Then she reconsidered. Yes, the man was a little overbearing. And, yes, he was obviously used to getting his own way. The rich and powerful usually did. On the other hand, she was extremely interested in seeing the rest of his famous collection. *Don't cut off your nose to spite your face, Christine.*

In the end she accepted, and they set off down the corridor toward a set of double doors that were marked: ART GALLERY.

As they approached, the tinted glass doors opened as if by magic. A slender, aesthetic-looking man was standing just inside the gallery. He gave a small bow and said, "Mister King."

"This is my special guest, Doctor Christine Day," Adrian said by way of an introduction. "Christine, this is Doctor Henry Davis, the curator here at the Royal Palace."

Christine recognized the gentleman's name. He was a highly regarded scholar and was considered *the* expert in the field of ancient Egyptian literature. "It's a privilege to meet you, Doctor Davis. I've read your work, of course, including your groundbreaking research into the literary texts of the New Kingdom period."

Henry Davis blushed with pleasure. "Thank you, Doctor Day. And may I return the compliment. It's not every day I have such a distinguished visitor to the gallery."

Once the pleasantries had been exchanged, Adrian glanced down at the gold watch on his wrist and said politely, but firmly, "Since it's after hours for the gallery, we won't keep you, Doctor Davis. I'll show Doctor Day around myself, and I'll make sure the guard locks up when we're finished."

Henry Davis gave a nod and wished them a good evening. Then it was just the two of them.

The gallery was comprised of six areas arranged like spokes on a wheel. Each area was lighted and situated so the artwork on display was shown to its best advantage. Christine was amazed by the diversity of Adrian King's collection: The paintings, sculpture, and other artifacts covered more than three thousand years and several cultures, not just ancient Egyptian.

As they made their way from exhibit to exhibit, Adrian strolled beside her, tall, dark, and enigmatic. *And* utterly charming. This was a man who knew how to work a room, how to work people, especially women. Tiny fissures in her nerve endings sent out a warning. It was a warning Christine chose to ignore.

"When did you learn to speak ancient Egyptian?" she inquired after several minutes.

"As I mentioned before, I've studied many languages," Adrian said, as they paused to admire a watercolor by Henry Salt depicting a scene in the tomb of Seti I at Thebes, painted circa 1818.

It was an answer of sorts, Christine supposed. Not that she was surprised to find out he was multilingual. Adrian King was reputed to have a world-class education as well as a brilliant mind, and, according to rumors that surfaced every now and then, a ruthless streak that could strike terror in the hearts of grown men.

They stopped in front of a mahogany case filled with jewelry. Christine lingered over one particular amulet of pale green faience in the form of the circular *shen* sign symbolizing infinity, eternity, and protection. "This is one of the finest examples of a *shen* hieroglyph I think I've ever seen," she said, suitably impressed.

Adrian indicated the next display case. "Then you will also appreciate these ouroboros amulets."

"The snake that bites its own tail," she said, more to herself than than to the man standing beside her.

"As you know, the ouroboros and *shen* symbols are of particular importance in jewelry design and tomb adornment," he said, leaning over to gaze at the fine gold pieces inlaid with semiprecious stones. "Especially when held in the claws of Horus or Nekhbet as they offer eternal protection to the king."

Christine had to hand it to him, he certainly knew his Egyptian mythology.

Then, while Adrian was busy studying the ancient amulets, she took the opportunity to study him.

He wasn't handsome in the conventional sense, she decided. His features were too strong and too uncompromising to be summed up by a word as mundane as *handsome*.

His jaw was emphatic. His mouth was sensual. His skin was the color of a hot desert sun as it reflected off ancient temples and age-old monuments. An air of power clung to him like a second skin. He radiated self-confidence and self-assurance. He exuded a raw masculine sexuality and a seductive promise of passion for any woman he might take an interest in.

As a matter of fact, Adrian King was *the* quintessential male in the prime of his life.

Christine found herself wondering how old he was. He appeared to be in his mid to late thirties, but there was something about him that seemed almost ageless. She had to admit she was intrigued; an emotion few men had ever aroused in her.

Who are you really? That's what she wanted to ask Adrian. *And how did you acquire such a vast and valuable collection of Egyptian antiquities when they're strictly policed and rarely, if ever, fall into private hands?*

Circumstances had been entirely different back in her great-great-grandfather's day. Archaeologists, treasure hunters, wealthy collectors, even tourists were allowed to return home with whatever artifacts they discovered in the Valley of the Kings, at the temples at Luxor and Karnak, at the magnificent rock-cut temples of Abu Simbel, or purchased on the street corners of Cairo. Those "souvenirs," including hundreds, perhaps even thousands of mummies, ultimately accounted for most of the Egyptian antiquities exhibited in modern museums around the globe, not to mention Cleopatra's Needle in New York's Central Park and a similar ancient obelisk that was presented to the British nation in 1819 and resided along the Thames Embankment.

By the late nineteenth and early twentieth centuries, foreign archaeologists were permitted to take away with them only half of what they had unearthed. But that soon changed as well. It was a different world now, with strict rules in place.

Rules were made to be broken.

Where had that thought come from? Christine wondered as her gaze settled on the impressive ring Adrian was wearing on his right hand. From her vantage point and under the unique lighting of the gallery, she could clearly see the ring. It was comprised of a bloodred carnelian scarab set in gold prongs and positioned above a cartouche of beautifully carved hieroglyphs, also rendered in gold. She couldn't read the name within the cartouche, but the ring appeared to be very old and expertly crafted.

She gave a mental shrug. That was the problem with gold. It was difficult, if not downright impossible, to determine its age. In fact, gold was considered the bane of any serious Egyptologist. It was a distraction and it never told you anything concrete.

Christine gave a small sigh and was about to move on to a display case filled with shabtis or small funereal statuettes, when Adrian stopped her and inquired, "Tell me, how did your great-great-grandfather happen to locate the cave and its artifacts?"

SEVEN

Christine thought it might be a good idea to preface her answer with a disclaimer. "You have to understand that I heard the account of what happened from my grandfather, and that it had been handed down to him from his grandfather." For a moment she allowed her mouth to curve into a nostalgic smile. "Both gentlemen loved to tell a good bedtime story."

Adrian was watching her intently. "And how did this bedtime story go?"

In her mind's eye Christine could see her grandfather's weathered face and hear his distinctive baritone as he told her one tall tale after another, swearing they were true, and insisting they were "family history." She still missed him, and she realized he had been on her mind since she'd stepped out of the taxicab and walked toward the entrance to the Royal Palace.

"It was a blistering hot day," she said, repeating verbatim the words Lawrence Day had used to begin his version of the story. "The sun was unrelenting. It was so hot that the fish of the Nile were said to have sought refuge on dry land and the birds of the air flew down and filled the sacred temples. The sun baked the desert floor until the earth itself cracked into shards like so many pieces of broken pottery; it beat down mercilessly on the caravan of donkeys and camels and men."

"I can't imagine that an experienced guide would have agreed to venture into the desert under such circumstances," Adrian said, as if he had firsthand knowledge of desert ways. "It's risky enough for those who know the dangers involved."

"Nevertheless, according to my grandfather's story, Clarence Day and his party insisted on riding out to the Valley of the Kings that day in spite of the heat," she said. "Several hours into their journey they stopped to rest under the welcome shade of an overhang. That was when my great-great-grandfather dismounted and started climbing up the face of a nearby cliff, much to the consternation of his fellow explorers and their guide, or so I was told. When several in the party shouted up to him, asking what he was doing, he called down to them that he had glimpsed an inscription etched into a rock wall above."

"And had he?"

"Yes, as it turned out, he had."

"Was it an ancient inscription?"

"My great-great-grandfather later judged it to be at least three thousand years old."

Christine could feel the tension in the man beside her; it was almost palpable.

Adrian turned and faced her. "Do you know what the inscription said?"

She bit her bottom lip and nodded. "As a matter of fact, I can recite it word for word." Then she started to speak in the ancient tongue: "'*And they did lay the great and powerful Merneptah Seti in his eternal home, and it was a palace rich beyond compare. And the way to the royal tomb was sealed and soon forgotten by all men.*'"

Adrian didn't move a muscle.

Christine continued. "Anyway, my great-great-grandfather noticed a narrow ledge wide enough for a man to stand on. He managed to hoist himself up onto the rock face and struggle to his feet. It was then he spotted a small opening in the limestone. That opening turned out to be the entrance to a cave."

Adrian frowned; a deep crevice formed between his dark blue eyes. "The same cave where the ancient papyrus and the other artifacts were unearthed?"

She nodded and launched into the rest of her story. "They were sealed inside earthenware jars that were buried under several millennia of sand and rubble."

Adrian looked coldly amused. "I see."

Christine wondered if the expression on his face meant he disapproved of the events of that expedition, or whether he simply wished he could have somehow gotten his hands on the artifacts himself. "This was long before antiquities were covered by international law, so my great-great-grandfather was permitted to bring his findings back to this country." She paused to moisten her lips and then ventured, "Of course, an avid collector like yourself would be well aware of the restrictions regarding antiquities."

Adrian shrugged his shoulders in that elegant way he had of moving his body. "Most of mine are reproductions."

"But not all."

"No, not all. I've been fortunate enough to acquire some genuine pieces through the proper channels," he said.

Christine was quite certain he could produce the provenance and the paperwork to prove he was the rightful and legal owner of each and every artifact on display in the Royal Palace. A man in his position couldn't be too careful.

Still, there was talk. There was always talk about the rich and the super rich, she reflected, and Adrian King definitely fell into the latter category.

They walked on and it was another minute or two before Adrian casually inquired, "What happened to the other objects Clarence Day found on that expedition?"

"Our family eventually donated them to the Oriental Institute at the University of Chicago, where they're still exhibited and available for study." Christine looked up and was surprised to discover they had exited the art gallery and were now standing in a secluded hallway in front of an elevator marked PRIVATE. Apparently the guided tour was over. "Thank you for showing me your collection, Adrian."

"It was my pleasure, Christine."

He took her hand in his, and a jolt of awareness—more like an electric shock—singed her fingertips, shot up her arm and across her chest, before spreading to her neck, her face, even her scalp, leaving her tingling from head to toe.

In addition, her throat was suddenly bone dry. Parched. The tiny hairs on the back of her neck seemed sensitive to the slightest movement of the air around her. Her senses were heightened, intensified, on red alert. She had to fight an almost overwhelming urge to jerk her hand back, to turn tail and run.

Adrian didn't seem to notice her increased agitation. He turned and entered a code on a digital keypad and the elevator door silently glided open.

"The casino at the Royal Palace is impressive in its own way, especially when it's viewed from the crow's nest. Perhaps you'd like to join me there for a glass of wine," he said.

Christine couldn't think of a single reason why she shouldn't accept his invitation—except for the warning that kept sounding somewhere in the deepest and darkest recesses of her mind: *Danger. Danger, Christine. Danger.*

EIGHT

He was playing a dangerous game.

Was there any other kind worth playing?

Inviting an Egyptologist—especially one who was an expert on Merneptah Seti, on *him*—into his private world, into a world he fiercely guarded, a world he kept concealed, hidden, shielded from all eyes, was either very daring or very foolish, Adrian thought as he stood gazing out over the crowded casino.

Inviting the woman he had seen countless times in his dreams, the woman he had created the scented oil for, the woman he had extolled in an ancient love poem, the woman he referred to as the Beautiful One, into his *inner sanctum* without first knowing why she was here, was not only foolish, but dangerous.

Dangerous for her.

Dangerous for him.

For he was tempted to tell Christine everything, to confess that she had haunted his dreams for as long as he could remember, to ask if she knew him, recognized him, had seen him in *her* dreams.

You draw ever closer to insanity, to madness, Adrian. And she will surely think you mad if you blurt out the truth.

What was the truth?

If you believed utterly and completely, did that not become your truth?

One thing he knew for certain: The thought of having Christine near him sent a frisson of excitement racing along every nerve ending in his body. He had never felt so alive. Yet for both their sakes he should send her away, command her to leave his presence, exile her from his domain, put her out of his head and his heart. But he couldn't bring himself to give the order. At least not yet. He would have her stay if only for a little while.

Adrian took a drink of Pétrus and held the rich, complex taste of the Bordeaux on his tongue for a moment before swallowing. Then he turned to Christine. "Do you play?" He indicated the blackjack tables, roulette wheels, and slot machines in the casino below them.

"I'm not much of a gambler," she said, sipping her wine. "I don't like taking risks."

Adrian was tempted to remind her that life itself was a risk, then he thought better of it. By all the gods, it would be infinitely easier to carry on a conversation with the woman if he could tell what she was thinking and feeling. He nudged his mind closer to hers, but once again found himself thwarted by an impenetrable wall.

Christine's skill in blocking her thoughts and emotions appeared effortless. He wondered if she had learned out of self-defense or had been born with the ability. Or perhaps it was an involuntary response like breathing. In the end, he supposed it didn't matter. She was a mystery, a puzzle, a Pandora's box that he did not have the key to open.

Adrian watched as she stood and peered out the tinted glass of the crow's nest. "Are you looking for someone?" he inquired.

She shrugged as if she were indifferent to his curiosity and the tone of command in his voice.

"Would you like to borrow my binoculars?" He indicated a pair on the table at her elbow.

Christine didn't answer his question, but asked one of her own. "Is that what you do?"

"What I do?"

"Stand up here and watch through a pair of binoculars, lord and master of all you survey?"

She was nearly right. He was lord and master here, but he had no need of binoculars. They were strictly for show. His eyesight was far more acute than that possessed by any normal human being. *But you're not normal or human, are you, Adrian?*

"This is my world. I created it, and I like to keep a sharp eye on it," he said sanguinely.

" 'Eye in the sky,' " Christine said, putting her wineglass down and picking up the binoculars. She appeared to make a methodical search of the area around the craps tables. When she located the person she was looking for, Adrian could tell only by the slight stiffening of her shoulders and the small inhalation of air into her lungs.

"What is it?" he inquired over the rim of his wineglass.

"It's a friend of mine, a colleague who accompanied me to the Royal Palace tonight. I've spotted him at the craps tables." She hesitated, showing a rare moment of indecisiveness. "I told Bryce I'd catch up with him later."

Was this Bryce more than just a friend and colleague? Adrian wondered.

A wash of color flooded Christine's cheeks. "I think he may be in over his head," she said guardedly. "And I suspect he's had too much to drink."

Adrian opened his senses and inhaled deeply. He could smell wave upon wave of emotions emanating from the casino floor. The odors were familiar and unmistakable. Using his special abilities he narrowed his search to the craps tables, zeroing in on her colleague. He knew immediately the man had acted rashly and stupidly. He had lost a great deal of money in a short period of time. That was always the risk in a high-stakes, fast-paced game like craps, especially for the novice gambler. Or the overconfident one.

Adrian breathed in again, and this time he deliberately held the stink in his lungs. He could smell avarice and greed and deception pouring from her so-called friend like the sweat that was visible on his skin. And there was more, but the man's brain was clouded by the amount of alcohol he had consumed.

It went against the grain, but Adrian finally offered, "Would you like me to invite this friend of yours to join us?"

Christine swallowed hard and said, "Yes, please."

"Point him out to me," he said, keeping up the charade.

Christine handed Adrian the pair of binoculars and he held them up to his eyes, maintaining the illusion of needing them to see. "He's the tall, blond man in the pin-striped suit," she said.

Adrian felt his hackles rise. "And his name is?"

"Bryce St. Albans."

Adrian spoke into his mouthpiece. "Phelps, we have a guest I would like to invite to the crow's nest." He gave Eric Phelps a description and the man's location, and then added, "Tell Mister—"

"Doctor," Christine quickly corrected.

"Tell Doctor St. Albans that Doctor Christine Day is with me, and ask him to join us."

Phelps was quick. "And if the gentleman refuses, sir?"

Adrian knew there was no leniency in his tone when he said, "Make sure he doesn't."

Phelps understood. "I'll deliver him personally to the general, Mister King."

Five minutes later there was a discreet knock on the door of the crow's nest.

"Come," said Adrian.

The door opened to reveal the head of his personal security force and behind him, a little the worse for wear and a little unsteady on his feet, was Bryce St. Albans.

Adrian reminded himself it was time to play the role of host. "Doctor St. Albans, won't you join us?"

"Sure. Why the hell not?" came out in a slurred and ungracious tone of voice.

Adrian turned his attention to his security chief. "That will be all for now, General."

"General?" St. Albans's ears perked up. He turned and stared openly at the man beside him.

Adrian kept the introductions brief. "This is the head of my personal security, General Rahotep."

The man gave a slight nod of acknowledgment.

Bryce St. Albans laughed; it was a loud bray of sound. "Rahotep? Is that Italian?"

General Rahotep didn't so much as crack a smile. "No. It is not." He didn't explain further.

Now that he was in closer proximity to the man, Adrian found he could read Bryce St. Albans like an open book. He didn't like what he saw. The man was imbued with a sense of entitlement and self-importance. He was ambitious and willing to do whatever it took to succeed, even if it meant lying, stealing, cheating, or worse. St. Albans was guilty on all counts.

His heart is black and corrupted, Adrian thought.

Then another emotion surfaced: lust. Impure, unadulterated, and unholy lust that reeked of every crude, vulgar, unnatural, and obscene act that a man was capable of.

Could this profane desire be directed at Christine?

By the Great Sacred Eye, it must not be. It would not be as long as he drew breath, Adrian vowed, his mind reeling with the flood of emotions that surged through him. Christine Day was his and his alone.

And he protected what was his.

NINE

Bryce St. Albans was a fool.

And she was an even bigger fool for thinking that she had to protect Bryce from himself, Christine thought. And for agreeing to have Adrian invite him to the crow's nest.

She was mortified by her colleague's behavior. He was loud, obnoxious, rude, *and* drunk. He was embarrassing himself and her. She wished she'd left well enough alone.

You should have known better, Christine. You can't save everyone from themselves. That's always been your problem: trying to rescue people, especially the men in your life.

A burst of raucous laughter filled the lounge. It was Bryce. He was apparently under the impression that he'd made another one of his so-called witticisms. And he was helping himself to a glass of wine.

The man was worse than a fool. He was boorish and uncouth. He was downing the expensive, vintage Bordeaux as if it were cheap jug wine. Glass in one hand, red wine spilling onto the carpet underfoot, Bryce lurched forward and grabbed her arm, muttering something about needing to speak to her in private.

Christine was highly annoyed. "Let go of me," she said under her breath, trying to spare him—and herself—any further embarrassment. Either Bryce didn't hear her or he didn't care. When she tried to break free, he tightened his grip on her wrist.

It was at that moment she sensed Adrian and Rahotep coming toward them. Both men moved so quickly it took her breath away. They were lightning fast—like the strike of the sacred cobra, *iaret*, symbol of Lower Egypt, patron deity of Buto, often depicted as the Eye of Re on ancient tomb walls, and always shown in pairs as the guardians of the gates to the underworld.

Bryce was stunned. Within seconds he was sequestered on the opposite side of the crow's nest, arms pinned behind his back, razor-sharp pains shooting through his body, crystal wineglass gone, vanished, and Rahotep restraining him with one hand without so much as breaking a sweat.

He broke out into a cold sweat. "What the f—?" The pain increased; his arms went numb.

"Silence!" The command came from General Rahotep; it sounded like the hiss of a deadly snake.

Christine cringed. Didn't Bryce recognize the danger

inherent in these men? They weren't the usual garden-variety academics he could dazzle with his boyish good looks, his pithy conversation, and his list of fancy graduate degrees. Adrian and Rahotep were intelligent, sharp-witted, battled-honed in a way that her fellow professor and Egyptologist would never understand.

"The king was a warrior in those days, Christine." Her grandfather's words echoed in her head.

That's what these men were: warriors.

Then, without warning, Christine found herself in one of her "waking" dreams. It was evening once more. The air was still. The weather was balmy. The sky was star-filled. The only illumination was the light cast by a sliver of silver moon overhead; it bathed everything and everyone in a soft white glow. She and Adrian were floating in the pool of warm water surrounded by the living lotus plants and luxuriating in the aftermath of love making.

With a shout, Rahotep rushed into the courtyard, raising the alarm, sword drawn, chest armor in place, prepared to defend them from an enemy as yet unseen.

Adrian moved in front of her, using his own body as a shield to protect her. She could feel her breasts pressed against his back, her nipples—still tender and sensitive from his touch—scraping across his bare skin and sinewy muscle. She was still half-aroused: It was that fine line between violence and sexual desire. She melted into him. She wrapped her arms around him. She held onto him for dear life. But she wasn't afraid for herself. She was afraid for him. . . .

Christine blinked several times in quick succession

and found herself once more in the crow's nest, her body pressed against the back of Adrian's tuxedo jacket, her hands grasping his waist.

Her cheeks flamed scarlet. She stumbled backwards and said, "I'm sorry."

Adrian turned. "No apology is necessary, Christine." He looked her over. "Are you all right?"

She nodded.

He was solicitous. "Are you certain?"

She finally managed, "I'm fine."

Adrian didn't appear to be completely convinced. "How is your arm?"

She glanced down at her wrist. The imprint of Bryce's hand was clearly visible on her skin. She'd have bruises. "It'll be all right." She peered over his shoulder, trying to catch a glimpse of her colleague. "How's Bryce?"

She sensed the implacability in Adrian. This was not a man who would easily or quickly forgive his enemies. "He should not have grabbed you," he said at last.

"No, he shouldn't have," she said. "I do think, under the circumstances, we need to make allowances."

Adrian frowned in displeasure. "You don't have to make excuses for your colleague, Christine. He's a bully and he manhandled you. I have no time for a man like that."

Neither did she, Christine realized.

"Speaking of time, it's time I was leaving," she announced to no one in particular, but to all three men in the room. "I have an early seminar in the morning."

Adrian glanced down at his watch and then up at his security chief. "Is it dark outside, General?"

"It is, my king."

Christine's head came up. She must be mistaken. Rahotep must have said *Mister King*. "Dark outside?" she said eventually.

Adrian turned and gave her an explanation of sorts. "The sunlight bothers my eyes."

"You're photosensitive," she concluded.

"Yes," was all he said. Then he turned to his security chief. "We will be escorting Doctor Day and Doctor St. Albans back to the university. Please arrange for a car to be downstairs at my private entrance in ten minutes."

"I'll see to it immediately," Rahotep replied.

"You will assist Doctor St. Albans since he seems a little under the weather." The man was a master of understatement. "Doctor Day and I will follow shortly."

Once they were alone, Adrian took her hand in his and gazed into her eyes, mesmerizing her with his words. "I would like you to join me for dinner on Saturday evening, Christine. At that time I will show you my personal collection of Egyptian antiquities."

She had suspected all along that the best pieces weren't in the public lobby downstairs or in the art gallery. "I'd like that very much," she said, her voice a little breathless.

"I'll send my driver for you at eight o'clock."

"I'll be ready," she said.

Adrian offered her his arm. "The car is here for us."

She wondered how he knew.

Adrian must have read her mind. He pointed to the tiny headpiece in his ear. "The miracle of modern technology."

"Of course," she said, remembering he'd spoken to someone named Phelps earlier.

Still, something niggled at Christine. Something she'd seen out of the corner of her eye or at the edge of her peripheral vision. It hadn't registered at the time, but now she recalled those few moments when Adrian had been watching Bryce through the binoculars. She'd known what he was thinking: St. Albans was a fool, a weakling, a poseur.

He was right, of course.

And, just for an instant, she'd had the impression that Adrian could have seen the other man even *without* the binoculars.

Christine shivered; she was suddenly covered with gooseflesh. More than ever she wanted to ask Adrian: *Who are you really?*

TEN

"What do you think of St. Albans?" Adrian said to Rahotep as the two men stood on the terrace of his penthouse, gazing out at the blaze of lights that was Las Vegas at night.

Rahotep stated his opinion. "He is not a warrior."

"No, he isn't." Adrian took a drink from the glass of water in his hand. Only a desert dweller, which he had always been, could truly appreciate the gift of water.

Rahotep continued. "St. Albans cannot hold his liquor. He gambles away that which he can ill afford to lose. He does not show the proper respect for the females of his kind. He is not honorable. And I see—I feel—no strength in him."

"Nor do I." Adrian took another drink of water and savored its clean, sweet taste. Then he added, "I don't trust him."

Rahotep laughed. It was a sound more akin to disdain or contempt, yet it was as close to laughter as he ever came. "We don't trust any humans."

"That is true, General."

There was a minute or two of silence.

"I could make him disappear, my lord."

Adrian appreciated the sentiment behind his friend's offer. "I know you could."

The former head of his armies was dead serious. "No one would ever be the wiser. No trace would ever be found. St. Albans would simply vanish from the face of the earth."

Adrian knew Rahotep was always true to his word. "Regrettably, his disappearance would upset Doctor Day. Not to mention the authorities."

Rahotep gave a nod of his head, indicating that he understood making the man disappear was not an option.

"We will, however, keep a sharp eye on St. Albans," Adrian said as he loosened his formal necktie. He undid the top two or three buttons of his white dress shirt, then dispensed with the gold cuff links at his wrists, before rolling his shirtsleeves up to the elbows. Once he was comfortable, he took a deep breath and held the night air in his lungs. Between the proliferation of men and machines crowding the city streets below and the constant stink of human emotions, he could detect only a hint of the vast desert that surrounded them. "Sometimes I miss the Black Land," he admitted to his fellow soldier.

Rahotep stood beside him. "As do I."

"And the old ways."

"There was much to recommend the old ways," Rahotep said in agreement.

Adrian filled his glass from a crystal carafe on the table at his elbow. Even here in the middle of the Nevada desert, water could be had on demand, at the mere touch of a button or the turn of a faucet. As much water as he needed, as much as he wanted, as much as he desired. "Still, this land and this life have many advantages," he said.

"Indeed, they do," Rahotep concurred.

Once again there was silence between himself and the general, as there often was.

In days long gone, silence had routinely been required on the battlefield. It was a key tactic in the stealth attacks and the element of surprise they had used so effectively in defeating the enemies of the Black Land.

It was also the silence between two men who had known each other since the moment of their births. Adrian had been only six days old when his cousin was born. They had been raised together, schooled together, trained together, and fought together.

Then there had been the silence of the grave, the tomb, the sarcophagus: They had both spent millennia without hearing the sound of a human voice.

Since his awakening, followed not long after by Rahotep's, their silence had been of a different kind. As important as words were to an ancient Egyptian—they believed that words had power beyond anything that these modern humans could comprehend—there were thoughts and feelings that were beyond words. By a mutual, unspoken agreement, neither of them felt the need to fill that silence with meaningless chatter.

Ironically, there was never silence in the casino thirty stories below them, Adrian reflected. It was a continuous racket of sound. By design, the hotel lobby of the Royal Palace, with its lush carpet, neutral palate of colors, and serene surroundings, was separated from the noisy gambling area.

Adrian finally broke the silence. "I sense danger approaching, Rahotep."

"I have sensed the same, my lord."

Adrian's eyes darkened. He felt power surging through him like a narcotic. "I was the first to awaken."

"That is as it should be, as it was ordained."

"You were the second."

Rahotep snapped to attention. "It is my duty and my privilege to stand guard over you, my king, whatever time or place you choose to reside in."

Adrian acknowledged the general's loyalty. "I have dreams. Dark dreams. And I have suspected for some time now that others have also awakened."

Rahotep's nostrils flared. "They have not come forth. They have not made themselves known to you. They have not prostrated themselves at your feet and paid the proper homage. They have not begged for your forgiveness. They hide behind these modern trappings and disguises." Venom dripped from his voice. "They are cowards."

Neither of them spoke the word *traitors*.

"No doubt you are right, Rahotep."

The general gave no quarter. "I do not fear them. I will be ever vigilant. I will destroy the enemy."

"This time the enemy will be the awakened, will be our own people," Adrian said, facing the bitter reality of the battle he knew was to come. "Blood of our blood will be spilled."

Rahotep was the ultimate pragmatist. "Blood is blood. The rivers will run red with it. The earth will be drenched by it. The air will stink of it. That is the way of war. But we will fight side by side, as we always have."

Adrian clasped Rahotep's forearm in the salute of one soldier to another. "As we always have, General."

"I will allow no one—and nothing—to come between you and your destiny, my king."

And what was his destiny? Adrian wondered.

Christine.

Her name was a whisper on the desert wind that swirled around him. Yet when Adrian opened his heart and his mind and again took in the night air, it was only danger that he smelled.

ELEVEN

April in Paris.

She had chosen Paris that April ten years ago because of its ethnic diversity, because she could easily blend into a metropolitan city with millions of inhabitants and thousands of tourists, because it was the fashion capital of the modern world, and because there was a certain je ne sais quoi about the French and there always had been.

After all, it was the French, specifically one of Napoleon's army engineers, who had discovered the Rosetta Stone in 1799. It was also the Frenchman Champollion who had completed the translation of hieroglyphic writing by comparing it to the Greek and demotic script on the celebrated stone tablet, thereby opening up the ancient world to the modern. And it was the French who had dared to erect a glass pyramid over one of their most cherished landmarks, the Louvre.

She loved Paris and the Parisians, and they loved her back. She had that indescribable sense of style some Frenchwomen seemed to be born with. She had started out as a seamstress at one of the couture houses, but her extraordinary talent, not to mention her exotic beauty, had been noticed immediately, and before long she was designing for one of the more avant-garde establishments.

Her rise in the fashion industry was often described as meteoric, and she soon had her own label of haute couture called "Maya." Her name was synonymous with sleek, linear skirts and pants, tops and jackets of the finest linen or the softest leather, always paired with unique accessories, and always finished off with gold jewelry embellished with carnelian, turquoise, lapis lazuli, even colored glass.

The colors she chose were the colors of the desert: the golden sands of the Sahara, the yellow rays of the sun god, the white limestone pyramids once crowned with pure gold, the purple sunsets, the skies of vivid blue, and the oasis of green along the banks of the Nile. There was a subtle theme to Maya's designs: It wasn't blatantly Egyptian or pharaonic, and yet there was a quality that evoked another time and place, a time of myths and legends, pharaohs and god-kings, a place that was now known only in dreams.

Maya still dreamed of her life before her "awakening," although it seemed a distant memory, as if she were peering at her past through a finely woven fabric.

She was descended of kings and queens through the bloodlines of both her father and her mother, and had been a member of the royal household. Indeed, she had been cousin to the pharaoh (although in truth, he'd had many cousins) and had lived a privileged life at court until the time of the Betrayal.

The king's betrayal and her own.

Her culpability still haunted her. She had been a fool, what the French called an *âme damnée*—a damned soul, a dupe—and she had paid dearly for her foolishness.

Lately Maya's dreams had grown increasingly disturbing, *cauchemars* filled with visions of horror: rivers running red with blood, screams of terror, most often her own, but sometimes the echo of her mother's frantic cries for help, or her younger brother's fear. She awoke from her nightmares drenched in sweat, her heart hammering in her breast, her lungs starved for oxygen, feeling as if she were suffocating, gasping for air as if there were never going to be enough air to breathe again, the damp bedsheets twisted around her legs and torso. Oh, how like the ritual wrappings used by the royal embalming priests those constricting bedsheets seemed to be in the dead of night!

Of late she had noticed physical changes in herself that could not be explained away. Her fingernails grew many times faster then they had in the past; she had to trim them almost daily. Her sense of smell, her hearing, even her eyesight had grown so acute that she lived in a world dominated by her senses. There were even times when she looked in the mirror and imagined that her teeth, especially her incisors, were growing longer and sharper, almost pointed.

She took to wearing hats and gloves year-round; not as a fashion statement, but because she had developed an extreme sensitivity to sunlight. And she never went out without a pair of dark glasses protecting her eyes.

Then there was the hunger, fierce and gnawing, excruciatingly painful, that racked her body, making her double over and retch until her stomach was empty and she was spitting up blood and fluids from her own innards. The hunger was so intense, so all-consuming, so dread-filled that she feared for her sanity and her very soul.

She knew it to be *the* Hunger, and she was petrified of becoming what the ancients called an Eater of Blood and a Breaker of Bones, what these humans, these mortals, called a vampire.

What ridiculous stories human beings had concocted in the past few centuries—a mere pittance of time—about blood eaters, based on a culture that had produced a prince named Vlad Dracula, also called Vlad the Impaler, supposedly immortalized in a horror novel written by Bram Stoker.

Even using the word *culture* was laughable, for there had been no culture in this Dracula's principality, at least not by ancient Egyptian standards. These Transylvanians, these Wallachians, whatever they cared to call themselves, had been savages, primitives, barbarians with none of the elegance and beauty, none of the poetry or music or adornments that had been part of her world and her daily life.

As a member of the royal household, she had eaten only the choicest meats and the most exotic fruits. She had enjoyed the sweetest honey cakes and the freshest dates. She had been served only the best wines. She had lived a life of privilege with servants and slaves to wait upon her hand and foot, to fulfill her every wish, to do her every bidding. She had been answerable to only a few: the queen, Nefertari, while she lived; Prince Rekhmire, favored half-brother to the king; and, of course, the king, himself, Merneptah Seti.

Yes, these mortals had spawned crude legends and stories they labeled "vampire," while her people had long ago been creating literature of unbelievable grace and beauty, even about the demons, even about the Eaters of Blood and the Breakers of Bone, as they were described in the *Book of the Dead*.

Still, she supposed the result was the same in the end: The hunger of such creatures demanded feeding, required blood, someone else's blood, in order to survive.

Maya knew her hunger would soon have to be fed, the terrible thirst quenched. She also knew that would mean searching the streets of her beloved Paris until she found some poor soul no one would miss, someone she could sink her teeth into and drain dry. The chosen one would die, sacrificing his life, so that she might live.

What would that make her?

What would she become?

What of her heart? What of her soul?

She did not want to kill, but it was a matter of survival.

There was only one thing for her to do before it was too late. She must approach the king. She must beg for his forgiveness and solicit his help. She knew he had awakened decades before her: She'd seen his photograph in newspapers and magazines, and, appropriately, he was again a king, this time commanding a vast financial empire.

Perhaps Merneptah Seti—he now went by the name of Adrian King—would have the answers to her questions. After all, he had been the strongest and the wisest and the greatest of their people.

"Or perhaps he will have you executed on sight," she said aloud. It was possible he would not wait to hear why he had been betrayed, and how she had been betrayed along with him.

That was a chance she'd have to take, Maya thought. She was prepared to accept her fate—whatever that fate might be.

TWELVE

Christine was escorted to the private elevator by the strong, silent man who had ridden in the back of the limousine with her. He had given his name as Pollard and told her that he worked in security under General Rahotep.

She assumed Pollard was ex-military by his bearing, the buzz cut he sported, the perfect crease in his pants, and the weapon she had glimpsed underneath his tuxedo jacket.

Pollard was a man of few words. During the half-hour drive from the university to the Royal Palace he had made no attempt at small talk and had asked her only two questions: *"Would you like something to drink, Doctor Day?"* and *"Is the temperature in the vehicle comfortable for you, Doctor Day?"*

Her answers had been: *"No, thank you,"* and *"Yes, it is,"* in that order.

The elevator doors glided open with a soft *ping,* and Christine stepped inside. Pollard followed. He inserted a key into a special lock and then pushed an unmarked button on the electronic display panel. The elevator apparently went to one floor: the top floor of the Royal Palace, Adrian's penthouse.

Moments later there was another soft *ping,* and the elevator doors opened again, this time on the thirtieth floor. Pollard gave a brisk nod in place of a salute and wished her a good evening.

Christine walked into a marble foyer roughly the size of her apartment back in Chicago. The entranceway was nearly devoid of furniture. On one side was a gold table—she briefly entertained the thought it might be solid gold—and on the other side was a statue of a cat, sacred to the goddess Bastet, wearing a protective *wedjat-*eye amulet around its neck, gold hoops in its ears, and a gold ring in its nose.

But it was the walls of the foyer that were its main feature: They were covered with beautiful, hand-painted murals. The first depicted an idyllic landscape of date palms, fields of ripened grain, and a blue serpentine river Christine assumed was the Nile. There was a small boat with a white sail in the background, and in the foreground, figures of peasants working the fertile fields along the riverbank.

Another mural showed foreign rulers bringing tribute to the pharaoh, who sat before a table heavily laden with offerings of gold, jewelry, frankincense, and myrrh, and off to one side a bevy of princesses to be added to his harem. Alongside this panel was a second that portrayed the king as a great hunter. He was standing in his chariot and thrusting a long pointed spear at one of the wild bulls running in front of him.

The next scene showed common foot soldiers as they pursued lesser game in a field of reeds, and a flock of wild ducks flying out of a papyrus thicket, apparently having been disturbed by a crocodile lurking in the undergrowth.

The final mural pictured a lush, green islet, and at its center, a sacred lake and a small temple. According to the hieroglyphic inscriptions above the pylon, the temple was dedicated to Hathor, the goddess most often associated with sexuality and pleasure.

The double doors directly in front of Christine were gilded with more gold. The doorknobs were falcon heads, also gilded, and representative of the god Horus, god of the sky, embodiment of divine kingship and protector of the pharaoh.

As she approached, the doors to the penthouse opened and Christine found herself face to face with General Rahotep. She had expected to be greeted by a butler or the concierge, not the head of Adrian's personal security force. She quickly hid her surprise.

"Good evening, Doctor Day."

"Good evening, General."

"May I welcome you on behalf of Mister King."

"Thank you."

"Mister King has asked me to extend his apologies to you. His meeting with the prime minister ran longer than he'd expected. He is still showering and changing and will be late in joining you for drinks before dinner."

Christine was curious, of course, but she wasn't

about to ask *which* prime minister. "I quite understand," she said.

"May I offer you some refreshment while you wait?"

"Perhaps a glass of Campari."

"Sweet or bitter?"

"Bitter, I think," she said.

"With soda and ice?"

"Yes, please."

Rahotep excused himself for a minute and returned with the drink she had ordered. "Mister King also requests that you make yourself at home. Please feel free to go anywhere in the penthouse you like. There are many interesting objects to see."

"Thank you, General."

"Is there anything else I can offer you, Doctor Day?"

She graciously said there wasn't, and he promptly withdrew.

Christine slowly circled the vast room in which Rahotep had left her. One wall was nothing but glass display cabinets filled with dozens of pieces of art glass. She knew just enough to be impressed by Adrian's collection of Lalique, Chihuly, and Steuben.

At the opposite end of the room was a grand piano fit for a king or a palace, which Christine supposed described Adrian's penthouse atop the Royal Palace to a T. She'd never seen anything like the gilded Bösendorfer piano with its ornate carvings, again of the falcon-god Horus, on either end of the keyboard.

Sipping her Campari, she wandered into the adjoining lounge, and discovered a painting by David Hockney hanging above a sleek, modern fireplace. Opposite were several nudes from Picasso's Blue Period and a huge Cy Twombly canvas that covered nearly an entire wall.

Adrian was a man of expensive and eclectic tastes, she decided. Surprisingly, not everything in the penthouse was antique or ornate. In fact, most of the decor could best be described as clean and modern with deceptively simple lines.

Next was the library. It was wall-to-wall books on every subject from the classic Greek tragedies to quantum physics and string theory. Positioned around the room were overstuffed leather chairs, each with a matching ottoman, and each with its own reading lamp. It was a scene straight out of an English country house.

Down a short hallway from the library was the game room. There was a pool table in its center with an antique Tiffany lamp hanging overhead. Smaller tables were arranged around the perimeter for playing chess, backgammon, and hounds and jackals, a favorite of the ancient Egyptians. There was a wet bar in one corner and a collection of vintage slot machines in another.

Adrian lived very well.

Christine realized the penthouse must be thousands of square feet in size. For a moment she wondered how he would ever find her. But somehow she knew he would.

Then she caught a glimpse of what appeared to be a rooftop garden. She put her glass of Campari down on the bar and strolled outside. It was actually a giant greenhouse or conservatory with a retractable roof, which happened to be open. Christine looked up at the star-filled sky overhead.

Vegetation in the garden was lush and diverse: palm

trees of every size and description, tropical plants, of which she could identify only a few of the more common varieties: Hawaiian ginger, bromeliads with their unusual flowers, birds of paradise with their splash of vivid color, and orchids, fragile appearing and far more subtle in tone, and somewhere there must be gardenias growing. Christine could smell their distinctively sweet scent.

She paused by a tranquil pond filled with koi fish. They were a living rainbow in shades of orange and red and blue and green, and even metallic hues that appeared to be hammered from gold or platinum. When she dipped her fingers into the water, the koi came up and nibbled gently on her fingertips.

Adrian King had created an oasis—a paradise— thirty stories above the desert city below.

Christine heard the sound of rushing water and realized there must be a fountain or a waterfall nearby. She followed the telltale noise as it grew louder and louder. She left the natural slate pathway, skirted a thicket of giant ferns, and there it was in front of her: a waterfall, ten or twelve feet in height, cascading over a natural-appearing rockfaced cliff before plunging into a pool below.

She stopped dead in her tracks. Someone was standing under the waterfall.

A man.

A naked man.

Adrian.

He had his eyes closed and his face turned up as he luxuriated in the water pouring over his body. His arms were raised over his head. His hair was wet and slicked close to his scalp. His mouth was open as the water splashed onto his face.

Rivulets ran down his chest, along his waist, past his pelvis to the nest of pubic hair below before dripping off his genitals. Stimulated by the surging water, his penis was partially engorged and his testicles were round and full.

Christine's mouth went dry. She licked her lips and an image of her mouth on him, licking him, suddenly appeared in her head. There was a roaring in her ears. She was holding her breath, and she dared not take a breath.

She was becoming aroused herself. She could almost feel him inside her like a fire in the blood, like a long, hot line of pleasure from her head to her toes.

She should turn and leave. She was intruding. She was invading his privacy. But she couldn't seem to move . . . or didn't want to. She was playing the voyeur and yet she felt no shame in watching Adrian as he stood naked under the waterfall.

He was all muscled flesh and battle-honed arms and thighs. Broad shoulders and a narrow waist. Smooth bronzed skin except for a jagged scar across his chest very near to where his heart must be.

He was everything primal. Everything erotic. Everything male.

He was beautiful.

THIRTEEN

He was lethal.

This wasn't the kind of man that a woman got casually involved with and then went merrily on her way.

Who said anything about getting involved with Adrian King?

You already are, Christine, and you know it.

She'd never thought of herself as a gambler, as a risk-taker, and yet she was about to take the greatest risk of all: starting a relationship with a man she barely knew, a man who could have any woman he wanted, a man she saw in her "waking" dreams.

Just because she'd dreamed she and Adrian had made love—well, had sex while bathing in an ancient pool—didn't mean it was inevitable they would become lovers. And, yet, she believed in fate, she believed in that inexplicable world that came to her in dreams, and in that world this was the man of her dreams.

Adrian opened his eyes and looked straight at her. There was no surprise on his features. He wasn't startled by her presence, and he certainly wasn't shocked. It was almost as if he had known she was watching him.

As a matter of fact, he was behaving as if it were perfectly natural for him to be standing there nude, dripping wet, and partially erect, while she stood, fully clothed, a few feet away.

Without a word Adrian stepped out from under the waterfall and started toward her, moving with the power and agility of a great jungle cat in its natural habitat; it felt like an exotic jungle in the conservatory with the myriad plant life and with the roof open to the night sky.

His gaze never left her face. His muscles rippled, flexed, with a strength that went beyond the physical, although Christine knew instinctively that there were few who could match the physical strength of this man. His body was hot and tight. His eyes were blazing. The closer he got the more erect he became.

Christine tried to swallow and found that she couldn't. She tried to breathe and discovered she'd forgotten how. She couldn't seem to recall air ever going in and out of her lungs of its own volition. She considered running away, but couldn't find her legs.

Adrian walked in a direct line toward her until he was no more than a foot away. "Christine."

She'd never heard her name spoken in that tone. It wasn't a question. It wasn't a statement. It was some kind of elemental awareness. It was recognition on the most basic and primal level. He was commanding her, caressing her, seducing her with his voice.

"Adrian." She wasn't sure if she said his name out loud or only thought she did.

He took another very deliberate step toward her. He pressed his wet body to hers. She fell back an inch or two and found her spine scraping the bark of a tree trunk.

Adrian raised a muscular arm on either side of her head. He grabbed a sturdy branch in each hand for support. Then his body, hard and rigid and supremely confident, imprinted itself onto hers until she could feel the outline of every bone and muscle.

His gaze was fixed on her. His mouth hovered above hers. But he didn't kiss her. He didn't touch her with his lips or his tongue or even with his hands. He simply leaned into her, pinning her between his body and the tree. Stealing her breath. Her will. Her sanity.

Then he began to move and Christine heard a low animal keening, like a moan, in the lush tropical undergrowth, and it was some time before she realized the sound was coming from her throat, from her lips, from her. "Please, Adrian."

She was drowning in the azure blue sea of his eyes.

"Please?" His breath became the air in her lungs.

"Please . . ." She couldn't find the words. She wasn't sure she knew the words. How could she ask for something that she both desired and feared? Something she needed desperately, but something that might well be the death of her?

Adrian took a half step back and gave her breathing room, and she groaned in protest. Then he reached down and grasped her fingers in his. He turned her palms up toward her body and guided her hands as he traced a slow pathway from her neckline down the front of her dress, and across each breast.

Christine could feel her nipples puckering against the damp material, against her own palms. He took her index finger and teased each nipple with her nail, pinched each between her thumb and finger, tugged each into hard little points. The sensation of touching herself, arousing herself, but under his command, his control, made her wet in places that had until now been dry.

Then he guided her hand lower, across the quivering muscles of her stomach, along her waist, and lower to that sensitive mound between her legs. He hiked her skirt up so her dress was bunched into a wade over a low tree limb, and she felt the night air on her bare skin. He slipped her finger under the narrow scrap of silk, flicked it back and forth across silkier flesh until she arched her back and moaned. He inserted her finger and then slid his own in beside it, and suddenly she couldn't breathe, couldn't think, could only *feel*.

Throbbing. Aching. Pulse-pounding need. Hunger. Madness. Bright red behind her eyelids, followed by pitch-black. Shattering. Splintering. Then falling, falling, falling.

Christine sagged against Adrian, supported by his strength and the stalwart tree behind her.

It was some minutes before her mind cleared enough to realize that if she stepped away and looked into a full-length mirror, she would see the imprint of his body on her dress. Her breasts would show the outline of his chest, even the indentation of his male nipples above her own, making them hard and firm and tender to the touch.

Her waist would bear the imprint of their hands, the front of her skirt the same as he had cupped her at the apex of her thighs. Her dress would clearly indicate where his erection—large, hard, demanding, with no give to it—had been. Then the round and firm testicles, they would have left their mark as well.

It was all dampness underneath, saturating every scrap of clothing, every inch of flesh, inside and out. Everywhere. She was drowning in the aftermath of a sensual flood.

"Christine." He said her name again in that thrilling way that made her feel like a creature of the senses, of the night.

"Adrian." His name sounded like a cat purring; it vibrated in the back of her throat.

She took his hands in hers—his were so much larger, so much stronger, but he let her lead and he followed—and placed them on his body. She used his finger to trace the outline of his mouth, dragging it across his lower lip, then along his chin, down his neck and onto the muscular wall of his chest.

He had just enough nail to torment, to tease his male nipples with, to leave a light scratch on his skin from shoulder to shoulder, to entangle in the smattering of hair in the center of his sternum and trace that dark arrow lower to where his erection protruded between them.

Christine's heart was in her throat. The air was thick and unbreathable. She tried to think and realized it was futile. She was beyond thinking; she was going purely by feel.

She touched the tip of his penis with the end of his finger and it jerked in her hand. She wrapped his palm around the smooth hard shaft and covered it with her own. She pumped slowly at first, watching for the first dewy drops to appear. Then faster. And faster. And tighter.

She looked up and watched Adrian's expression before the inevitable overtook him. There was tension in his face, in the stiffened posture of his body, in the taut muscles of his abdomen and thighs. She could feel his body burning, aching, hardening to the point of pain, then building, climaxing, exploding.

At the last possible moment Adrian thrust his head back and parted his lips on a sound that seemed preternatural until she realized he was shouting, "Christine!"

FOURTEEN

He'd acted on impulse.

Something he rarely allowed himself to do, Adrian acknowledged as he tucked a strand of soft chestnut brown hair behind Christine's ear. Her appearance had been immaculate when she'd walked into the rooftop garden and found him bathing under the waterfall. Now her hair was down around her shoulders, all wet and wild, a mass of enticing curls. Her makeup, what little she wore, seemed to have vanished. Her dress. Well, her dress was ruined. It had been blue-green silk. Now it was splotchy and wrinkled and torn in several places.

He looked down. Her feet were bare. Sometime during the wonderful insanity of those moments in the conservatory Christine had lost her strappy high-heeled sandals.

Adrian liked her this way.

In fact, he preferred her this way.

Wet and wild.

Of course, this wasn't how he had intended to make love to her for the first time: standing up, with her back rubbing against the rough bark of a tree, branches snagging her dress, with her fully clothed while he was completely nude and in a painful state of arousal.

It's only the beginning, the first of many times you will claim her body, her mind, her heart and soul. That was the thought that went through Adrian's consciousness.

He reached for Christine's hand and, without any conversation, guided her through the gardens and into the master suite. This was a woman who was completely comfortable with silence; that alone made her a rarity.

There was not a word spoken, certainly no words of protest or false modesty on Christine's part, as he undressed her and dispensed with her clothing piece by piece. Scraps of silk fluttered to the floor, forming a damp pile at their feet.

Then she turned to him and with her fingertip traced the line of the jagged scar across his chest. He shivered, shuddered, felt his body stir, come to life again, harden. As a matter of fact, his erection had never really gone away, not even after he had reached his climax in the greenhouse.

Would it always be that way? Adrian wondered. Would he make love to Christine and then find that he wanted her again and again, and more than ever?

He recalled a conversation he'd had with himself long ago. In fact, it had been on the day of his death.

"You're a fool," he'd said in a whisper so that none

of those present in the royal chamber could hear him. He had been thinking about the woman who appeared to him in his dreams, the woman he called the Beautiful One, the woman who was his "secret." He'd told himself that she wasn't real, that she didn't exist, that she was created from his own imagination and from his loneliness. He'd even reminded himself that there was no perfect woman for him.

He had been wrong.

For she was here with him now, more than three thousand years after he had first seen her in his dreams.

This was the woman.

She was his destiny.

Christine bent her head and pressed her lips to the scar on his chest. "Does it hurt?" she asked.

"Yes." But Adrian wasn't thinking of his old battle wound; the one that had come very close to ending his life the year before his betrayal *and* murder. He had been thinking of those he'd trusted and of their treachery. He laughed, and he heard the darkness in his laughter and the memory of pain. "No."

Christine was a curious creature. She lifted her head and stared straight into his eyes. "How did you get the scar?"

He told her the truth. "I once served as a soldier. I was wounded in hand-to-hand combat."

Adrian heard the intake of air into her lungs. He saw her gray eyes go wide. "How frightening."

He didn't remember being afraid. He did remember the adrenaline pumping through his body, giving him the strength to ram his sword straight through the heart of his opponent, then watching as the shadow of death extinguished the life in the other man's eyes. He was dead before he hit the ground.

That was the reality of war: Some lived; some died.

He had continued to fight until the battle was won. By day's end—and it had been a very long day, indeed—he had been covered with blood, some his own, but mostly with the blood of countless enemies. It had not been until much later, once they were back in their encampment, that General Rahotep and his half-brother, Prince Rekhmire, had insisted that he allow a royal physician to attend to his wounds.

"I was not afraid," Adrian said, and realized belatedly that he had spoken aloud.

Christine gazed up into his face. "Did you kill the man who wounded you?"

It was so long ago. And yet the memory was fresh; he could still smell the carnage of the battlefield.

Adrian sighed. "Yes."

She gently pressed her lips to the spot directly above his heart where the scar tapered off into a thin white line. "I'm glad you're the one who lived," she murmured against his flesh.

Adrian snorted. "So am I." He'd been half afraid Christine was going to ask him if he had killed many men in battle. He had no wish to answer that question.

A soldier did what a soldier had to do.

As did a king.

But that was then; this was now.

Adrian had always had an imagination. Now his was running wild—for Christine was standing before him as he had often imagined her: a sensuous woman with a long elegant neck, beautiful uptilted breasts just the right size for his hand or his mouth, with ripe berry centers, so sweet tasting on his tongue, the nipped-in waist, the flair of her hips, wet hair dripping down her back, creating a tiny stream of water from her neck, along her spine, over the rounded and enticing derriere, only to disappear into that intriguing cleft between her buttocks.

He had dreamed more than once of making love to Christine out in the desert—his desert—under a full moon with moonlight washing over her body, her skin covered with granules of golden desert sand. He would have to brush the sand from her breasts, of course, and watch her nipples respond to the caress.

He would stretch out naked on the earth and she would straddle his hips, wrap her legs around his waist, lower her body inch by inch and impale herself on his eager and waiting flesh. He would fill her with excruciating thoroughness until she had taken every inch of him.

Then it would begin. Slowly at first, with a rocking motion. Followed by a thrust of her hips, then his. Then another thrust and another and another. Stronger. Deeper. Then deeper still.

Adrian could almost feel her, taste her. His penis was hard and pressed painfully between them. The pain of pleasure. The situation was explosive. If he thought one more erotic thought, if he touched Christine, kissed her, moved against her body, he was going to come again where he stood.

She could feel the incredible strength in Adrian's shoulders, in his arms, his chest, his thighs. She could also feel the control. This was a man in control of himself. She wanted to make him lose that control, Christine realized.

Why? was the thought that leapt into her head.

She who had always prided herself on her self-discipline and self-control, she who understood why a man like Adrian would want to maintain control of his life and of his world. Why would she want to make him, make herself, lose control?

Because you want this man to want you as he has never wanted any woman before.

She wanted Adrian to need her, desire her, hunger for her as he had never needed, desired, or hungered for anything or anyone in his entire life. She wanted to be the one thing that he couldn't buy no matter how much money he had. She wanted to be the one thing in this world that he didn't have the power to command. And she wanted to be the one thing that he had to have to live.

Christine took a step closer and tangled her arms around his neck. His hair was long, still damp, un-combed. It brushed back and forth along his nape with each movement of his head. She ran her fingers through the strands of his hair; they had the feel of black silk.

There was the slightest stubble on his chin and along his jawline; it was like fine sandpaper. Not that she was com-plaining. The sensation of his beard scraping her skin was erotic.

She opened her eyes and studied the dark arch of his brows, the suggestion of an aristocrat nose, the ears tucked close to his head. She knew from the other evening that his blue eyes had a rim of darker blue around them. Nearly blue-black. She was surprised she remembered.

At the time she hadn't thought that she had noticed such an insignificant detail.

Adrian finally opened his eyes and stared down into hers.

What did she see? Intelligence, certainly. Interest. Curiosity. Strength. Determination. This was a man who was used to being in charge of himself, of the situation, of those around him. Perhaps calling him *my king* hadn't been a slip of the tongue on Rahotep's part, after all.

The heat radiated from Adrian's body as if he had stored up warmth from the sun, and yet she knew he was sensitive to sunlight, and doubtlessly avoided it.

He smelled of the night and of the lush gardens. His mouth came down on hers, stole her breath *and* her reason away in a single heartbeat. He tasted of . . . the desert.

"You taste like the desert," she murmured, leaning her head back and looking up at him from within the circle of his arms.

"And what does the desert taste like?" Adrian asked her.

The only description she could come up with was, "You."

His hands cupped her breasts, which were pressed against his chest. Nipples tightened and became engorged. Sensitive to the slightest touch. Itchy, and itching to be pinched, licked, tongued.

Christine heard an aroused groan. It was her own. He could do so much to her with so little. It left her frightened and trembling and on fire for him, all at once.

Then his mouth blazed a white-hot trail along her

bare shoulder and across her collarbone to her other shoulder. He pressed his lips to the swell of her breasts. He moved lower and found her nipples, first one, then the other. He flicked his tongue back and forth across their sensitive tips until they were painfully tight and hard.

She untwined her hands from around his neck. She ran one hand slowly down each bare arm. She, too, could and would give him a taste of his own medicine. Her fingers roamed his upper body, teased the small, rigid male nipples, the hard muscles, the smooth skin, the smattering of hair in the center of his chest that formed a directional arrow down his torso, a direction that her hands naturally followed.

When she reached his waist, she felt his indrawn breath, his arousal so nearby, his suddenly rigid stance, and he moaned deep, deep in his throat. He wrapped his arms around her and lifted. She was aware of something smooth beneath her backside.

Where was she?

Then she realized they were stretched out in the middle of his oversize bed, and his hands were on her. His fingers were probing, insinuating, stretching, delving. She gave up thinking, heaved a long sigh that took her breath away and her resistance with it, realized her whole body was trembling and lay back, spread her arms, and tried to clutch the sides of the bed, but ended up with handfuls of luxurious sheets. He slipped between her thighs. She opened to him and the tip of his erection pushed against her.

She exhaled on his name. "Adrian."

"Christine," he said, his arms wrapping around her,

muscles primed, nearer and nearer, pushing against her, finding her.

Then he surged into her, and it was all searing heat and incredible friction and exquisite tension. He slipped in and out of her in a tortuously slow dance. She cried out his name, grabbed at his shoulders, sunk her nails into his flesh. Hot. Heavy. Burning. He filled her body and her mind.

He thrust harder, deeper, taking them both up and up, higher and higher. Skin sweaty and musky. Muscles strained to the limit. Hearts beating wildly. Hips pounding.

It was crazy and wild and terrifying. It was ethereal, beautiful, inevitable. Christine felt herself reaching for something that had always been just out of reach. Then she soared and called out her release. And Adrian followed.

Adrian spoke with the manager of one of the elegant designer shops down in the lobby of the Royal Palace and ordered half a dozen outfits delivered to the penthouse. He did so without first consulting Christine. There was no need to interrupt her shower, he told himself. Besides, he'd been able to determine her size at a glance. And he suspected her pride might get in the way of accepting a replacement for the green silk dress ruined earlier that evening.

The selection of clothing arrived shortly after his call and ranged from evening dresses to daytime suits to a diaphanous nightgown and bathrobe, all in a size six.

He picked up an in-house telephone and moments later room service was wheeled into the suite: platters of wafer-thin salmon, silver bowls of the finest Russian caviar, chilled lobster drizzled with Dijon sauce, steak tartare, sweet delicacies of nuts and dates and chocolate, all accompanied by bottles of his favorite wines: Château Lafite-Rothchild, 1985, and Château d'Yquem, 1975.

"You live very well," Christine said to him as she sat cross-legged in the middle of his bed, still wearing one of his bathrobes, the sash tied around her waist twice, nibbling on a piece of succulent lobster and sipping a glass of white wine.

Adrian stretched out beside her, relaxed, and helped himself to a morsel of dark chocolate, which he washed down with a drink of his favorite Bordeaux. "Yes, I do."

"Have you always lived so well?"

"Yes," he said without giving any details. "I enjoy being rich."

"Most people probably would," Christine said, laughing. It was unrestrained laughter. It was amused laughter. It was unrehearsed. Spontaneous. Delightful. Almost girlish.

Adrian listened to her laughter and soaked up the joyous sound. It was the first time he'd heard such innocent laughter in his penthouse high above Sin City, and somehow it made the luxurious suite feel like a different place, a place of peace. A home.

Later, they wandered through the apartment and he showed her his special treasures, including the beautiful and ornately carved chest with the simple lapis lazuli jar inside. Christine didn't realized its significance, of course. There was no reason she should. But perhaps someday, one day soon, he would tell her who he was.

Then he lost himself in making love to her again and again, staying inside her all the while, and gazing down into eyes that were the color of the sky at dusk.

And, for a little while, there was no past. No future. No dreams. No nightmares. No danger lurking in the back of his mind, gnawing away at his peace of mind.

There was only Christine and there was only now.

FIFTEEN

Christine awakened from a dead sleep with the taste of blood in her mouth. She reached for a tissue from the box on the bedside table and pressed it to her lips. Then she swallowed the fluid pooled in the back of her throat; its metallic taste burned from her esophagus all the way down to her stomach.

Her first thought was she must have bitten her tongue.

Her second thought: Where was she?

For a moment she was disoriented. Then she remembered: She was in Adrian King's penthouse. In his bedroom.

In his bed.

She blushed when she thought of all the ways they had made love, pleasured each other, enjoyed each other during the long, sweet night. It was everything she had ever dreamed of and more. Adrian had even vowed to her at one point that they'd always been meant for each other. She had wanted to believe him at the time. But would she still believe him in the clear light of day?

It was dark in the suite except for a thin slice of moonlight infiltrating through a slit in the blackout drapes, which covered the extensive wall of windows opposite the bed. She turned toward Adrian. She couldn't see anyone next to her. She reached out and found his side of the oversize bed was cold and empty.

Christine pushed herself up onto her elbows and peered down at the pile of pillows under her. She only hoped she hadn't gotten any blood on the expensive bed linens, although there were certain to be telltale stains from their lovemaking, a prospect that hadn't seemed to bother Adrian in the least.

Why would it? He probably spent more on a pair of sheets than some people earned in a year.

She recalled reading an article once in a magazine about the lifestyles of the rich, the famous, and the royal. Twelve-hundred-thread-count sheets, similar to the ones on Adrian's bed, were listed at $14,000 per pair, and that didn't take into account the fact that his wasn't a standard-size bed. It wasn't even a regular king or a California king. It was custom-made, as everything was in his top-floor apartment.

The man lived very well, indeed.

Where was he?

Christine got out of bed and reached for the bathrobe Adrian had ordered from the designer shop downstairs in his hotel complex. She'd never worn anything so beautiful, so soft, or so luxurious next to her skin. She could only guess what the robe must have cost since all the price tags had been discreetly removed before the clothing had been delivered to the penthouse.

Or maybe they were the type of clothes that weren't even marked with a price—as in, "If you have to ask how much it costs, then you can't afford it."

It was surreal.

This isn't the real world, Christine, she reminded herself.

At least it wasn't the real world as she knew it. It certainly wasn't the world she'd grown up in or the world in which she lived. She belonged in academia. Hers was a pursuit of knowledge, not wealth or material possessions. She was a professor and a scholar. It's what she did; it's who she was.

Like her grandfather and his grandfather before him, her passion had always been the study of ancient pharaonic Egypt. She had known for some time now that her passion would not include a husband or a family of her own. Those were the things that she had put aside, put away, much in the same way that women used to put fine embroidered linens in a hope chest for some day.

Sometimes someday never came.

Voices.

Christine could hear voices. A man's voice. Adrian's. And then a woman's voice: softer, pleading, crying.

Barefoot, and without making a sound, Christine slipped into the darkened hallway between the master bedroom and the library. There was a light on inside the book-filled room. The massive door was slightly ajar. She tiptoed closer and caught a glimpse of Adrian pacing back and forth, dressed in pajama bottoms and a bathrobe. There was a beautiful and exotic woman sitting on the floor, balanced back on her heels, her head bowed in a posture of obeisance.

Who was she?

Why was she practically kissing the ground at Adrian's feet?

The atmosphere in the library was charged with emotion; the air was thick with tension.

Adrian pointed an accusing finger at the figure. "You were the instrument of my destruction," he said in a tone that sent ice water rushing through Christine's veins. He was fearsome. Condemning. Unbending. With no latitude. And no forgiveness.

"I know, my lord," the young woman barely managed to say in a whisper.

"Why, Maya?" There was anger and anguish in his voice.

"Because I was a fool. A dupe. The traitors swore they would kill my mother and my brother if I did not help them." The lovely creature looked up and there were tears streaming down her face. "They were executed, anyway. Right before my eyes."

There was not the slightest sign of sympathy in his voice or softening in his manner when Adrian declared, "The untrustworthy can never be trusted."

A slightly defiant chin came up. "A lesson I learned the hard way," she said.

"As did I," he countered with bitterness.

Again, tears brimmed in the dark soulful eyes. "I beg of thee, beloved."

Adrian stopped her with a killing glance. "You will never refer to me in that intimate fashion again."

The young woman's forehead immediately sank to the carpet at his feet. "Forgive me, my lord," she pleaded. "It was a careless slip of the tongue. My only excuse is I'm desperate. I am beyond desperate. I am half out of my mind. I don't know what to do, where to turn. I need your help."

Adrian wearily rubbed his hand across his eyes and then, with a gesture of futility, admitted to the supplicant kneeling in front of him, "I have nothing to offer. I cannot help you."

The exotic creature raised her head a fraction, but she dared not look him in the face. "But surely as the strongest and the wisest and the greatest of our people, you have the answers."

He sighed heavily and shook his head from side to side. "I have no answers, Maya."

She seemed to slump forward, grow smaller, thinner, become enshrouded. "Then I am doomed."

"We are all doomed," Adrian stated.

It wasn't just his choice of words or his tone of voice—frightening as both were—that drove Christine to retreat into the darkened master suite. It was the young woman kowtowing at his feet. There was something between Adrian and the girl he called Maya. Something personal. Something intimate. Something that made Christine feel like an outsider, and an utter fool.

How could she have fallen for the oldest line a man used to seduce a woman: *You are my destiny*? She'd always been so careful not to let anyone get too near. And here she had slept with Adrian King—a man who could have any woman he wanted—on their so-called first date.

Christine felt tears gathering in the back of her throat, but she wasn't going to cry. She was mad. Mad at herself and mad at Adrian. And she was going to get the hell out of here just as fast as she could.

She quickly dressed in her own clothes, although they were damp and impossibly wrinkled. She made her way out of the penthouse and into the private elevator. Five minutes later she was hailing a taxicab and giving the driver the address of her room at the hotel.

SIXTEEN

Adrian knew Christine was gone the moment he walked back into his bedroom.

It *felt* empty.

He couldn't hear her soft breathing. He couldn't detect her distinctive perfume: the ancient oil he had created for her himself. He could see the sheets were thrown back, the pillows were in disarray, and the bed was vacant without turning a light on.

The clothing he had sent for was hanging in the closet; the door had been left ajar. There was a hanger dangling on the doorknob. Christine's green silk dress was missing.

But it was more than any of these things. He could sense she was gone; he could feel it. It was as if his apartment were suddenly as cold and as lonely as the grave. Any warmth, any joy, any love had vanished with her. There was even something missing in the very air he breathed.

How strange, and how ironic, Adrian thought, that he couldn't smell Christine's emotions or read her thoughts, and yet he knew immediately when she wasn't there.

"Where are you, Christine?" he whispered to the night.

He paced back and forth, then wandered through one dark and empty room after another, but he knew the search was futile. She wasn't in the penthouse.

Why had she left without a word?

There was only one logical explanation—if emotions could ever be characterized as logical. She must have awakened and heard him speaking to Maya.

"*By all the Hounds of Hell,*" Adrian swore in the ancient language, slamming his fist against the doorjamb in frustration. "You are a fool! An imbecile! You should never have consented to give Maya an audience while Christine was in your home."

He rarely made a mistake, but this had been a colossal one.

There was little doubt in his mind that Christine had eavesdropped on the damning part of their conversation and had not stayed around long enough to hear him tell Rahotep to escort Maya to a suite of rooms on the floor below this one.

What was Christine thinking?

What was she feeling?

By all the gods, he wished he knew.

Adrian felt more alone than he ever remembered

feeling in his entire existence. He was flooded with emotions. But they weren't someone else's, they were *his* emotions.

Stunned, he stopped dead in the middle of the pitch-black library. He breathed in the scent of parchment and ink and leather. He was aware of being surrounded by the wisdom of the ages. And he realized that he felt more like a man—more like a human—than he had in three thousand years.

SEVENTEEN

"Well, well, well, aren't you the dark horse?" came a smarmy masculine voice from the other end of the hallway. Then there was a guttural laugh—the kind that wasn't in the least bit funny or contagious—followed by the sound of breaking glass.

Christine was fumbling in her handbag for her room key, but her mind was a million miles away. She paused and peered into the shadows. "Who's there?"

Bryce St. Albans stepped into the harsh glare cast by the overhead light. His blond hair was tousled. His face was unshaven. There were dark circles under his eyes. His pants were uncharacteristically creased and his shirttails were hanging out. It appeared he'd been sleeping in his clothes. He wasn't wearing any shoes or socks, and barely missed the broken glass on the floor at his feet.

"I must say, Doctor Day, you look a little the worse for wear," he said.

There wasn't any way to conceal the fact that her silk dress was ruined. But Christine was in no mood for Bryce's sarcasm. "The same might be said of you," she shot back.

The man glanced down at the front of his white dress shirt, noticed the dark splotch between the third and fourth buttons, studied it for a moment, and then tried to brush the stain away with the back of his hand. "Must have been the Cabernet sauce at dinner," he mumbled as if that made perfect sense.

Or the Cabernet wine he had obviously consumed with dinner, Christine thought.

Bryce looked up at her, gave her the once- *and* twice-over, allowed his gaze to linger on her breasts until she felt like slapping him across his handsome face. A face, she realized, that was on the verge of becoming ugly, dissipated.

There was no mistaking the nasty innuendo in her colleague's tone when he said, "Was it raining earlier?"

Bryce knew darned well it hadn't rained. In fact, it was a perfectly clear, star-filled desert night.

Christine held her head high. "No. It wasn't."

He made a wild, uncontrolled gesture. "You look like you might have fallen into one of the fancy fountains out on the Strip. Your dress is all wrinkled," he said, stating the obvious.

She wasn't going to dignify that comment with a response. It wasn't any of Bryce's business what she had been doing or who she had been doing it with. Still, her face went hot.

She certainly had no intentions, of course, of telling her fellow professor that she'd had an encounter tonight with a very wet and a very naked man.

Is that what it was, Christine? An encounter?

"I heard through the grapevine that you had dinner with Adrian King this evening," came the slurred words. It seemed news traveled fast in university circles.

"Yes, I did."

Bryce swaggered toward her and she could smell alcohol on him from a good five or six feet away. It was as if the man had deliberately drenched himself in it like cheap cologne. "Taking up with the rich and famous now, are we?"

She refused to be goaded into saying something she would regret later. "Adrian King was kind enough to show me his collection of Egyptian artifacts."

Bryce took a step toward her and tripped over an nonexistent hump in the carpeting. He managed to catch himself before he fell flat on his face. "I'll just bet he was."

It occurred to Christine that her colleague might be jealous. Since Bryce had never shown any interest in her as a woman, that couldn't be the reason behind his sudden jealousy. But it was well known in academic circles that he was ambitious. Extremely ambitious. Perhaps even ambitious to a fault. Bryce St. Albans was definitely the type to consider meeting with Adrian King a huge feather in his cap, not to mention advantageous to his career.

Christine's temples were starting to throb; she could feel a headache coming on. "I'm sure if you want to see Adrian's collection, he'd be happy to show it to you."

Bryce snorted; it was not an attractive sound. "With you acting as intermediary?"

That wasn't what she'd meant.

He staggered forward. "I know for a fact that Adrian King doesn't show his personal collection of antiquities to anyone outside his intimate circle."

Sometimes finesse was the better part of valor. "He's a very gracious host."

"Exactly what did you have to do, Christine, in order to gain access to the inner sanctum?"

She put her shoulders back, mustered all the dignity she possessed, and looked down her nose at him.

Bryce didn't seem to notice. He snickered under his breath. "Or does the old saying apply here?"

Naturally Christine had no intentions of asking what the old saying was.

Bryce told her anyway. " 'Rode hard and put away wet,' isn't that how the expression goes?"

Her hand connected with his face before she had time to stop and think.

Bryce's eyes flew wide open. He raised his hand to his cheek where the imprint of her hand was clearly visible. "Ouch. That hurt," he whined.

She didn't feel the least bit sorry for him. "It was meant to. You were deliberately being insulting."

He backed off immediately. "I'm sorry, Christine." The apology seemed sincere. "I was acting like a jerk."

"Yes, you were."

He got that sloppy and familiar grin on his face. "Can we please let bygones be bygones?"

"All right." But she was exhausted and she did not want to be having this conversation with Bryce. Not now. Not ever. "I'm tired." She turned back to the door of her hotel room and inserted the key into the lock. "I'll see you at the luncheon tomorrow."

Bryce was beside her before she could close the door. "Would you care to join me in my room for a nightcap? It would be my little way of apologizing."

"Your apology has been accepted. Now goodnight, Bryce," Christine said firmly, shutting the door in his face.

She bolted the hotel room door behind her.

EIGHTEEN

Blood.
He could smell it. As a matter of fact, it had been the distinctive odor, the tantalizing scent, the ravenous hunger for blood that had awakened him.

He had been confused at first. Then he realized that he was still in his tomb, and that the voices he heard were men talking, hatching·their plans, in the outer room of his burial chamber.

He listened. Then he understood, comprehended. They were grave robbers.

Desecration.

Sacrilege.

Blasphemy.

It was strictly forbidden for anyone to enter this place where he had been laid to rest. To do so was to invite the wrath of the gods, to incur their extreme displeasure, to bring down damnation upon one's soul, to be eternally cursed.

Yet weren't you cursed while you still lived?

The memory of the time before his death: the time of his conviction, his imprisonment, then his execution and unceremonious burial filled him with rage, for he had been treated no better than a mangy cur that roamed the dusty streets scrounging for a scrap of garbage to eat.

He had been met not with adoration and respect and reverence as befit his station, but with disdain, disgust, even violence. He had been labeled a traitor and treated like a common criminal. Little wonder those memories were still fresh in his mind and in his heart, and made him see the world through a drenching rain of red.

He could feel his incisors growing and extending past his other teeth and over his lips, pointed, razor sharp, dripping with a caustic acid, and he knew what he was: He had awakened as an Eater of Blood and a Breaker of Bones.

The grave robbers were the first he drained dry and left as nothing more than a few scattered tibia and a hunk or two of indigestible hair. But they were as nothing. They were less than nothing.

He had acquired a hunger—an addiction—for human blood.

That hunger was easy enough to satisfy. Life was cheap in many parts of the world and there were always humans no one missed, no one gave a second thought to.

Or even a first thought, for that matter.

He fed upon the homeless, the weak, the feeble, the innocent, the naive, the reckless, the unwise who walked alone down dark and deserted streets at night.

But that soon became boring, mundane, horribly predictable. He needed to make a game of it, challenging himself to find prey that required the intelligence and the skill he brought to the hunt.

He added another element to the game by stealing the riches from another tomb—one that was yet to be discovered or desecrated when he ransacked its treasure. Then he entered their modern society as a playboy, luring women and men into his bed. By day he was a man of wealth, of education, of privilege, a thrill-seeker who raced million-dollar speedboats. By night he became a predator, a feared assassin, the ultimate Dr. Jekyll and Mr. Hyde.

His choice of avocation seemed ironic to him at first: that a man of the desert would crave being on the water. The attraction of speed he understood: It was thrilling and it made him feel alive again.

The object of the game, of course, was to push the limits and set no boundaries. He did whatever he wanted, whenever he wanted to, and the cost to these feeble human beings be damned. For surely they had been put on this earth for his amusement.

He soon discovered that like any addiction, he needed more and more excitement to satisfy his needs and desires. He must not, after all, be content to rest upon his laurels. Some might say he was in a downward spiral of self-destruction. They were fools. He felt a man—a god—was never more alive than when he was risking that life.

Besides, he couldn't die.

That was the laughable part. He was invincible. He was untouchable. He was immortal.

Of course, there had been that one close call nearly a

year ago. He had been going for a new speed record, pushing himself and his boat to the absolute limit of its power. At just past three hundred miles per hour, the engine had caught fire and the boat had started to break apart. He'd acted quickly, saving himself, for death by fire might be the one death even he could not escape.

He was aware that others like himself had awakened. But he wanted nothing to do with them, not even Maya, whom he knew lived in Paris, not far from his residence in the principality of Monaco. He owned several other properties on the Mediterranean as well. It seemed he could never bear to be too far from the water.

Yes, there was plenty of time to reacquaint himself with the other Awakened—after all, he had time, all the time in the world to make himself known to them. For now he would maintain his disguise . . . and wait for the right time.

He had plans for the game to end all games. Yet he was in no hurry to bring those plans to fruition.

"Vengeance is mine," Seth whispered to himself, as he slipped into the jacket of his hand-tailored tuxedo, tucked a few thousand into his pocket, and headed to the elite casino down the street with its crystal chandeliers and expensive champagne and delicious human beings just waiting for him.

NINETEEN

Christine came hurrying out of the university lecture hall, her leather briefcase tucked under one arm and her award plaque under the other, and ran directly into Adrian King.

She pulled herself up short.

Adrian removed the pair of dark sunglasses covering his eyes. Rather reluctantly, she thought. But then he was supposed to be sensitive to light or allergic to sunlight or something.

"Congratulations on your award," he said with excruciating politeness. "It's well deserved."

"Thank you," she said stiffly. She was as uncomfortable as she could ever recall being.

Adrian went on to compliment her. "Your acceptance speech was gracious, witty, and intelligent."

Christine managed to keep her mouth from dropping open. "You heard my speech?"

He nodded. "I slipped into the back of the lecture hall just before the ceremony began."

There was a moment or two of awkward silence.

Adrian put his shoulders back and seemed to force himself to say the words. "I also came to apologize about last night, Christine."

She moistened her lips before responding. "You don't owe me an apology."

Adrian frowned. "An explanation, then."

"You don't have to explain anything to me, either." She tried to walk around him, to circumvent this whole embarrassing situation, and ran straight into him for the second time in less than a minute.

The man moved like lightning.

Adrian lowered his voice to an intimate level. "You left without saying good-bye."

"I don't like good-byes," she tossed back. "Besides, you were busy." She might as well have come right out and admitted to him that she'd eavesdropped on his private conversation.

Adrian looked at her squarely. "I had important family business to attend to. My cousin arrived late last night from Paris. Her visit was . . . unexpected."

"Your cousin?" Christine knew she sounded skeptical. She didn't know whether to believe him or not.

"My cousin Maya. Perhaps you've heard of her."

She shook her head. "Is there any reason I should have?"

Adrian only hesitated briefly before saying, "Maya is well known in some circles."

Christine heard herself asking him, "And what, pray tell, might those circles be?"

"She's a fashion designer for one of the couture

houses in Paris. In fact, Maya has her own line of clothing, accessories, and jewelry. But she can tell you more about herself tomorrow evening." He quickly went on to add, "I know she's looking forward to meeting you."

"What is tomorrow evening?"

"I'm extending an invitation to both you and Doctor St. Albans to join Maya and myself for the show at the Royal Palace."

"Invitation accepted." It was Bryce St. Albans speaking. Christine had been so intent on her conversation with Adrian that she hadn't heard her colleague's approach.

"Well, I don't know . . ." she hemmed and hawed. "Our conference concludes tonight and there is so much to do before we fly home to Chicago."

Bryce looked at her like she had taken leave of her senses. "Are you kidding? *The Book of the Dead* is the hardest ticket to get your hands on in Vegas. It's sold out for something like the next two years." He turned back to Adrian. "That's very generous of you, Mister King, especially considering my abominable behavior the other night. By the way, I hope that's all water under the bridge now."

Adrian made a casual and dismissive gesture in the air with his hand. "Don't give it another moment's thought, Doctor St. Albans. We all make our share of mistakes."

Christine was suddenly suspicious. Something wasn't right here. In fact, something felt very wrong.

"I'll send my limo for the two of you, then. Shall we say nine o'clock?" Adrian reached out to shake St. Albans's hand.

"Tomorrow evening at nine," Bryce agreed cordially as he took his leave of them.

Christine opened her mouth to refuse his invitation for a second time. "Adrian—"

He cut her off. "I must go now, Christine, but it's imperative that you come tomorrow evening."

"Imperative?"

"I can't explain here. Or now. But you must come," Adrian said, slipping the dark glasses back into place and turning up the collar of his suit coat.

Then he reached into his pocket and removed something. Christine couldn't see what it was. He pressed it into her palm and closed her hand around the object.

"Until tomorrow night," he said, then turned and hurried out the door of the lecture hall and into the waiting limousine at the curb.

After the vehicle had pulled away and disappeared into traffic, Christine opened her hand and looked down at the object Adrian had given her.

It was the gold ring with the bloodred scarab that he always wore on his right hand. She held it up to the light and studied the name within the cartouche, the name she hadn't been able to make out before. Her heart began to pound in her chest.

The hieroglyphs clearly spelled out the name of Merneptah Seti.

TWENTY

"It's ironic, is it not, Rahotep?"

"What is, my lord?" the general said as the two men stood in front of the large-screen television in the game room of the penthouse. They were watching a special presentation on one of the documentary channels: It was the excavation of a recently discovered royal tomb from the Nineteenth Dynasty.

Adrian explained. "If my body had been prepared and embalmed after death as my father's was before me, and if I had finally been wrapped in fine white burial linen and placed in my sarcophagus, I would be as these mummies are today: excavated, x-rayed, poked and prodded, examined under a microscope, catalogued, and then exhibited in a museum somewhere." Adrian's brow creased into a deep, thoughtful frown. "Not exactly the 'eternal life' our ancestors had in mind."

"I see what you mean," Rahotep responded. He was a brilliant tactician on the battlefield, but he left the nuances of philosophical discourse to others.

Adrian reached up and rubbed a hand back and forth along his jawline. "In a perverse kind of way, the traitors did me a favor."

Rahotep stiffened beside him. "How so, my lord?"

Adrian clicked off the television. He'd seen enough. "When Maya came to you that night more than three thousand years ago with the warning that there was a plot to desecrate my body, you had no choice but to quickly take me away to my tomb without the usual rituals or embalming."

"That is true, my lord." Rahotep paused and appeared to consider for a moment the consequences of that night of stealth and secrecy. "Do you believe the story Maya told you yesterday?"

"Yes, I do." Adrian believed her, although he was not ready to forgive her.

Maya had been a fool—worse than a fool—and they had both paid the price. The ointment—one of the seven sacred oils—was the chosen method of assassination. A fortunate choice in the end since the potion was cleansed from his body as he slept, counteracted by the magic and the power that he had taken to his grave with him.

Yes, poison had been the weapon of destruction as Adrian had concluded after his "awakening," and it had been the death of him and the death of her. The traitors had lied to Maya and had refused to give her the promised antidote, which was the least of their lies. They had also murdered her mother and her brother and made her watch.

At least his royal cousin had done as he had commanded her, Adrian thought. She had made certain the lapis lazuli jar was with him in his sarcophagus. And he knew from Rahotep that Maya was the one who had warned the general of the traitors' intentions of cutting him into pieces as Seth had done to Osiris, and scattering him to all corners of his beloved Black Land. In that part of their plan, the traitors had been foiled.

And, in the end, he had died and he had lived again as it was ordained for him as king.

Rahotep was thinking along the same lines. "Since you, the king, were not embalmed according to our customs, all who were sworn to serve you, to protect you, all who honored you, all who loved you, also chose not to follow the ancient burial rituals."

"Consequently, I was able to awaken and to live again," Adrian pointed out.

"And once you had awakened, I followed," Rahotep said.

"Now others have awakened and followed as well." And like many dreams, Adrian realized, the dream of eternal life was one that could rapidly turn into a nightmare. For some of those who had awakened were traitors and they would not rest until he was destroyed once and for all.

Still, he would do it all again even if it meant spending only one night with Christine.

"I am weary, Rahotep." It was a signal that he was ready to retire and to be left to his own company.

"I bid you goodnight then," the general said as he nodded and made a strategic exit.

* * *

Later, Adrian opened the drapes in his bedroom and stood at the window, gazing out at the night.

If he looked past the neon brilliance of Las Vegas to the desert beyond he could see that the moonlight gave an eerie, iridescent glow to the distant landscape. Just past the sprawling city and its suburbs was a long stretch of nothingness. In his mind's eye, Adrian could see beyond the nothingness to a place high in the mountains, a place where he had long dreamed of building a home.

He unlatched one of the windows, leaned over, and rested his elbows on the sill. Then he inhaled deeply: The air was brisk and refreshing and held no memories for him.

He'd forgotten how quiet the night could be in the desert, and he remembered another desert halfway around the world and three thousand years in the past. He had slept out under the stars and listened to the faint whistle of the wind through the smallest scrub brush. The drone of insects somewhere off in an oasis of palm trees. The rare song of a night bird. The rustling of a creature skittering its way from one sand dune to the next. The occasional splash of a fish in the nearby Nile or the slither of snake or a crocodile.

Life seemed—*was*—simpler, more basic, back to earth and down to earth in the desert, which was one reason he knew he would return to the desert in the end.

Sometimes a man had to go back to his origins and deal with who he was.

"Who are you, Adrian King?" he whispered as he

turned and studied his reflection in the glass. "What do you want?"

He knew what he didn't want.

He didn't want to keep looking back at the past forever. A past that included betrayal, treachery, treason, and death. It was all ancient history now, anyway.

He didn't want to end up a shadow of the man he had once been. He did not want to become a creature of the night, an Eater of Blood and a Breaker of Bones. He would act before that time came.

Adrian shut the window, drew the drapes, and stretched out on the bed. He reached over and turned off the lamp on the bedside table. He stared into the darkness and the darkness stared back at him.

He drew the night air into his lungs and permitted it to permeate every cell of his body. He allowed his eyes to shut. He breathed in again. His eyes flew open.

Evil.

Suddenly he could smell it.

TWENTY-ONE

Candy snapped the gum in her mouth as she painted another coat of glossy polish on her toenails. Naturally she had been very careful to place a small cotton ball between each of her toes before she started. It wouldn't do to smudge a color like Pink Passion. That was one of the first things they taught you at beauty school: Smudged nail polish was a sign of a second-rate manicure or pedicure.

Besides, pink was her signature color.

She stopped snapping her gum long enough to ask a question. "How come we haven't heard from our employer? I thought he had another job for us."

Jason punched at the pillows behind his head and took a swig of beer from the bottle in his hand. "If I told you once, I told you a dozen times, Candy, the guy said he'd call when he was good and ready to call and not before. So quit your bitching."

"I wasn't bitching. I was just wondering." She bent over and blew on her toenails. "I was hoping we could take some of the money he owes us and go out for a real night on the town. Maybe get tickets to the hottest show in Vegas."

"Do you even know what the hottest show in Vegas is?" Jason said without looking up from the TV screen.

"Sure," she said around the next snap of her gum.

Jason turned his head. "Oh, yeah. If you're so smart, then tell me what is it?"

"The hottest ticket in town is *The Book of the Dead*. It's been playing over at the Royal Palace for more than a year. I hear you have to know somebody who knows somebody who knows Mister King himself if you want to get a ticket."

"Is that so?"

"Yeah," she said, sticking her tongue out at him.

"Well, considering that we were thrown out of the Royal Palace and told never to set foot in the place again, I'd say our chances of seeing *The Book of the Dead* are dead in the water."

Candy pouted. "That's too bad. I would kill to see that show."

TWENTY-TWO

Maya sat in the darkened theater and watched *The Book of the Dead* unfold on the stage below. As a designer, she was fascinated by the costumes and sets: They were sumptuous, richly textured, jewel-toned, and breathtaking. As someone who had lived through the events depicted by the actors and dancers, the acrobats and musicians, she was mesmerized and strangely spellbound by what she saw. As a woman, she was brought to tears by the love story.

But it wasn't her love story.

It was the love story of an ancient pharaoh and the woman who appeared to him in his dreams, the woman he treasured above all others, the woman he called the Beautiful One.

Maya knew Adrian King—Merneptah Seti—was the

pharaoh. Just as she knew that she was *not* the woman he had loved in the past or loved in the present.

She had suspected there was someone special, even millennia ago. They all had. Every female in the royal household had hoped to be singled out as the pharaoh's favorite after the death of his chief wife, Queen Nefertari, but no one was ever granted that privilege. Now she understood why.

How could any flesh and blood woman hope to compete with a dream?

Tears streamed unchecked down Maya's face. She wasn't usually so emotional, but tonight the past and the present had collided right in front of her eyes. And she wondered—doubted—if she had a future. She heaved a long sigh. Her makeup was going to be ruined. She was foolish not to have brought some tissues with her.

Then somebody in the seat next to hers pressed a tissue into her hand. Maya turned her head. It was Christine Day. Tears were streaming down her face as well, but Christine didn't seem to care what tears did to her makeup, possibly because she wore so little of it.

Maya mouthed, "Thank you."

Christine gave her a watery smile and silently formed the words, "You're welcome."

Maya looked back at the stage, but her attention had shifted to the man and woman sitting on either side of her. She'd been wondering all evening since the moment they'd been introduced, what the relationship was between Adrian, Christine Day, and Bryce St. Albans. Adrian had informed her that two professors— Egyptologists of all things—were in town for a conference and that he had invited them to the theater as his guests.

But there was something else going on here. Maya could sense it. She could smell it.

She didn't like Bryce St. Albans. Two or three times during the evening he had pressed his leg suggestively against hers and then pretended it had been an accident.

The man was a liar.

She'd always been able to read men like St. Albans, even in ancient times, even before her death and awakening. There was no great mystery to most males. They were obvious. They lacked subtlety and intelligence. They were simple creatures, really.

When a group of half-nude female dancers had appeared on stage during the performance tonight, St. Albans's odor had become downright unpleasant, disagreeable, offensive. It assaulted her senses, filled her nostrils, clung to her skin until Maya wanted nothing more than to excuse herself, dash from the theater, return to her hotel room, and take a long, hot, cleansing shower.

Why would Adrian want to have anything to do with a loathsome man like Bryce St. Albans?

Maya didn't know the answer.

But perhaps she was asking herself the wrong question. Perhaps the right question was: What did Adrian want with a woman like Christine Day?

There was a slight movement to Maya's left. Without turning her head she watched out of the corner of one eye as Adrian reached over and offered Christine the elegant silk handkerchief from the pocket of his tuxedo. A small gesture for most men, but a magnanimous one from a king. And Adrian was still very much a king.

Maya was intrigued.

She leaned closer to Christine, closed her eyes, and breathed in deeply. If she focused, if she concentrated, she could tell what these human beings were thinking and feeling, even the females, although they were always more of a challenge for her to read than the males.

Nothing.

Except a subtle whiff of an ancient oil, a distinctive one that Maya had never smelled before.

She tried a second time, breathing deeper, holding the air in her lungs longer, pushing herself harder until she realized she was getting dizzy and starting to hyperventilate.

Again, nothing.

Maya was puzzled. Apparently there was more to Christine Day than met the eye. She studied the other woman surreptitiously. She supposed some men might find her subtle features, her luxuriant chestnut-brown hair, and her slender body attractive. She knew there were even a few discriminating men who might value the woman's intelligence. Adrian had made it clear to her that this professor, this Egyptologist, was a woman of great intelligence.

That's when it hit Maya. How other men might feel about Christine Day was irrelevant. It was Adrian—it was Merneptah Seti—who was captivated by her.

What if she had been drawing all the wrong conclusions? Maya thought. What if it wasn't the other woman's physical attractions or her intelligence that intrigued Adrian? What if, like herself, he couldn't smell her thoughts and emotions?

What if Christine Day was the only human being Adrian couldn't read at will?

That would make her endlessly fascinating to him.

Maya's heart sank to her feet like a dead weight. It would explain so much, including his complete indifference to her as a woman, perhaps even his anger when she had used a long-ago term of endearment and called him "beloved." He had said he had nothing to offer her. He had stated that he had no answers for her, that they were all doomed.

Last night Adrian had been telling her the truth.

Maya realized that there was nothing for her here in Las Vegas. In fact, the sooner she packed her bags and flew back to her beloved Paris, the better.

Whatever the future held, whatever answers were out there for her, Maya knew she would have to find them for herself . . . in her own time and in her own way.

TWENTY-THREE

"I'd like a word with you, St. Albans," Adrian said to the other man as the four of them strolled out of the Royal Palace Theatre following the late-evening performance.

His guest nodded. "Sure. Glad to."

"Doctor St. Albans and I will catch up with you in a minute," Adrian indicated to Christine and Maya who were already being greeted at the door of the private owner's lounge by uniformed waiters: The first was offering glasses of champagne, the second a tray of sandwiches, and yet a third a delectable choice of petit fours.

"Incredible show. Stellar performances." Bryce St. Albans was gushing. "I wondered if there were going to be any girls in *The Book of the Dead*." Here he paused and winked knowingly. "Happy to say I wasn't disappointed."

"Girls?" Adrian repeated the word very deliberately.

Bryce lowered his voice, as if he were speaking as one man of the world to another. "You know. Showgirls. Scanty costumes. Bare breasts. G-strings. Nude dancers."

Adrian's mouth started to turn up at the corners. What an absurd little worm St. Albans was. "Surely nudity is a natural part of life."

"Maybe where you're from." His guest laughed; it was a loud bray of a sound. "But I can tell you that in my neck of the woods we don't see a lot of it outside of seedy strip clubs."

Adrian realized he would never care to venture into St. Albans's "neck of the woods."

"It was damned sporting of you to invite me to the show tonight, King. I'll tell you, everyone back at the conference was jealous," Bryce went on to expound to his host.

Adrian bristled at the uninvited familiarity. No one was permitted to address him as anything less formal than *Mister* King, with the single exception of Christine. But since it served his purposes, he forced himself to continue the conversation with this ridiculous human being. "Am I correct in assuming that you made certain they all knew you were going to be my guest?"

"Of course. After all, what's a little name dropping among friends? Wouldn't want to miss the chance to impress a few of the right people along the way. You scratch my back, I'll scratch yours. I think you know what I'm talking about. A man of business like yourself no doubt has useful contacts in many parts of the world."

"That is true." Although perhaps not in quite the way

Bryce St. Albans assumed. Adrian decided to let the man hang himself with his own rope.

"Well, it's no different in the field of Egyptology. If you want to get ahead, if you want to make a name for yourself, you've got to publish on a regular basis. You have to take advantage of every opportunity that comes your way. Of course, it also wouldn't hurt to make a spectacular find, but those are few and far between."

"Not that many royal tombs left to ransack in the Valley of the Kings?" Adrian suggested.

"Exactly." Bryce caught himself in the nick of time and said in a serious tone, "As professional archaeologists we try not to use words like *ransack*."

Adrian arched a dark brow. "What words do you use, then?"

Bryce pulled on his shirt collar as if it were suddenly one size too small for his neck. "*Discover*. Or *excavate*. Or *unearth*."

"I see." Indeed, he saw far more than Bryce St. Albans would ever suspect. "Since new tombs are few and far between, what about new theories?"

The man's face brightened immediately. "Yes. A new theory is almost as good if it's groundbreaking."

"So, borrow a little here . . ." Adrian supplied.

His guest nodded.

"Steal a little there," he went on to suggest.

Bryce smiled slyly. "I knew you'd understand."

"I understand perfectly." There was an underlying menacing tone to Adrian's voice that could not be mistaken for anything but what it was: a threat.

St. Albans started to look around nervously. "Maybe it's time we were joining Christine and Maya."

"We will as soon as we clear up one or two little matters." Adrian dropped any pretense of cordiality. "I know you to be a cheat and a fraud, St. Albans."

The man standing in front of him opened and closed his mouth soundlessly.

Adrian went on. "I have a security tape showing that you cheated at the craps table in my casino the other night."

St. Albans sputtered, "I didn't cheat."

"I have absolute proof that you did." Then he delivered the *coup de grâce*. "Cheating in Nevada is a felony."

"I only took a twenty-five-dollar chip from the other guy's stack," the fool blurted out.

Adrian set the record straight. "It doesn't matter if it's two dollars or five thousand dollars, it's still considered a felony. We take cheating very seriously in this state."

"I was under the influence," Bryce said, attempting to excuse his behavior.

"Doesn't matter," Adrian countered, shaking his head. "A man shouldn't drink if he can't hold his liquor."

Bryce lost all color. His face was blanched; bloodless. "I'll be ruined if this gets out."

"Yes, you will."

"I'll lose my tenure."

The man was worried about tenure? He still didn't understand the gravity of the situation. "That's not all you could lose."

Bryce snapped his fingers. "What if I give it back? Maybe we could locate this other guy through the same tape and I could return his twenty-five dollars. Or heck, I could pay him double for his trouble and give him fifty or even a hundred."

"You can't buy your way out of this." Adrian was tempted to squash the worm under his foot, but he had other uses for St. Albans. "I understand you're about to have a groundbreaking book published on the New Kingdom dynasties."

Bryce was caught off guard by the sudden switch in the direction of their conversation. "What?"

"I hear it's a real tour de force explaining your brilliant theories about the relationship between the various members of the royal families by a study you supposedly made of their DNA."

It was the word *supposedly* that got his attention, just as Adrian had intended it to.

Bryce started looking around for the nearest exit. "It's actually a theory any number of Egyptologists have been working on. I just happened to be the first one to put it all together in a coherent form."

"So you were the first?"

Bryce squirmed. "Well, several of us were working on similar ideas simultaneously."

"Several of you, including Christine Day?"

"She might have added a premise or two," he said, dancing around the issue as fast as he could.

"Only a premise or two?"

"Okay, maybe she was closer to being a collaborator." Sweat was forming on Bryce's forehead.

"I assume as a collaborator Christine would share the credit for this groundbreaking publication, and she would receive her half of any financial rewards."

A drop of sweat slid down St. Albans's nose, hung there for an instant, and then lighted on the lapel of his tuxedo, leaving a telltale blotch behind. "That could be arranged."

"It will be arranged."

Bryce took out a handkerchief and mopped at his face. "How do you know so much about my business?"

Adrian set his jaw. "I don't give a damn about your business, St. Albans. But I have made it my business to know anything and everything that has to do with Christine Day." He gave it a moment or two to sink in. "Have I made myself clear?"

"Yes, sir."

"She is under my protection now. Anything you do to Christine, you are doing to me."

"I understand, Mister King."

"For your sake, I hope so." Adrian knew he sounded at his most powerful, his most regal, his most formidable. "I do not wish to upset Christine or ruin this evening for her. So when we join the women for a glass of champagne, you will behave like a perfect gentleman. Is that understood?"

Bryce tried to swallow and say yes, but could only manage a slight nod of his head.

"After a few minutes, you will pretend to receive a telephone call and excuse yourself. You will politely step over to the other side of the lounge and act as if you're speaking with your publisher."

"Speaking with my publisher," Bryce repeated as if he were memorizing his instructions.

"When you return to the party, you will inform the rest of us that regretfully you must take your leave. There is a problem that requires your immediate attention. You're needed back in Chicago to go over some glitches in the final proofs before the book's publication."

"I have to get back to Chicago right away," Bryce said aloud as if he were starting to believe the story himself.

Adrian added, "You will catch the red-eye tonight. You will make sure that due credit is given to Christine Day. You will never cheat her or anyone else again."

"I won't. I swear I won't," the sniveling human promised.

Adrian was dead serious when he said, "If you do, I promise you I will know."

Bryce looked like his blood stood still.

"There is one more condition. If you ever set foot in Las Vegas again, I'll have you arrested."

"Believe me, wild horses couldn't drag me back here," Bryce St. Albans declared fervently as if he had an inkling of just how narrow his escape had been.

TWENTY-FOUR

■ "Like rats deserting a sinking ship," Christine muttered under her breath as Bryce set down a full glass of champagne, excused himself, and left the lounge.

Or she should have said: *a* rat.

Not that she believed for a minute that Bryce St. Albans had such pressing business back in Chicago that he actually had to catch the red-eye tonight.

It was something else entirely. Something Adrian had said to him while the two men were talking privately after the performance. *But it's really none of your business, Christine,* she reminded herself.

"I, too, must be bidding you good evening and goodbye," Maya spoke up a short time later. "Or as we French say: *au revoir.*"

Christine was surprised by her announcement. "You're leaving Las Vegas?"

"Yes. I'm flying back to Paris tomorrow. I have a new fall collection to design, models to approve, fabrics to choose." Maya gave an exaggerated sigh, and then said with a small smile, "You know what they say: A designer's job is never done."

Christine was determined to be polite. She held out her hand. "It was nice meeting you, Maya."

But Maya would have none of that. She graciously accepted Christine's handshake, and then reached up and bestowed a kiss on first one and then the other of her cheeks. "That is the way we do it on the continent."

"A lovely custom," she agreed. If they perhaps had met under other circumstances—at another time and in another place—she might have become friends with Adrian's cousin.

"I will say good-bye to you here as well, Adrian," the exotic woman said as she went up on her tiptoes and touched her lips very briefly to his jawline. Christine wasn't certain skin even touched skin since Maya seemed half-afraid of offending him.

"Good-bye, Maya," Adrian said without reciprocating the gesture. "I hope you have a safe journey home." Then he added a blessing in the ancient language: *"May nothing evil have power over you. May the eye of Horus be your protection."*

Maya responded in kind. *"May the Great Eye watch over you, my king."*

Then she was gone, and it was just the two of them in the private theater lounge with a wait staff of three standing by.

Adrian made a dismissive gesture in their general direction. "You may all go now."

The last waiter out the door closed it behind him.

Christine gave a self-conscious laugh once they were alone. "Well, you certainly know how to clear a room, Mister King."

"The waiters are unnecessary since you've scarcely eaten a bite of food and your champagne is untouched," he said, sounding reasonable about the whole business.

Christine was hoping he hadn't noticed. "I wasn't hungry." She planted a neutral expression on her face.

"Or thirsty, apparently."

"Champagne always seems . . ." Christine paused and searched for the right word.

"Celebratory?" Adrian suggested.

She moistened her lips before saying, "Exactly."

Adrian hesitated, then shook his head slowly. "This doesn't feel much like a celebration, does it?"

Christine wasn't going to lie to him. "No, it doesn't."

"Nevertheless, I'm glad the others have gone. I want . . . I need to speak to you alone," he said, rising to his feet, and starting to pace back and forth.

Maybe this was the imperative reason she was here tonight. That was the word he'd used yesterday afternoon at the university just before pressing the gold ring into her palm: *imperative.*

"That reminds me," Christine said, opening her handbag and digging around in the bottom for a moment. "I should return this to you." She held out the ring to him.

Adrian stared down at the cartouche ring, but did not take it from her. Instead he inquired, "How did you find tonight's performance of *The Book of the Dead*?"

"It was truly magnificent," Christine said without reservation. "I can understand why the show is sold out for the next several years. I've never seen such a beautiful interpretation of ancient Egyptian mythology, beginning with Seth's betrayal of Osiris, and his salvation at the hands of his beloved Isis. And then the story of the great pharaoh and the woman who appeared to him only in his dreams."

Adrian paused and gazed at her with those mysterious blue eyes of his. "There were tears on your face."

"Yes." In fact, there was still a huge lump lodged in her throat. It was the reason she hadn't been able to eat or drink. She had been so moved by the tragedy and triumph of the love story unfolding before her eyes that she could scarcely breathe.

"Do you believe ancient myths and legends are actually based in fact?" he said.

His question surprised Christine. "Are you asking me as an Egyptologist or as a woman?"

Adrian was clearly taken aback. Apparently it hadn't occurred to him that there might be two options available to her in answering his question. "As an Egyptologist," he said, picking the first choice.

"As a scientist and as an Egyptologist, I understand that myths and legends were handed down from one generation to the next in the form of oral history or stories, told around campfires or braziers or while huddled in tents in the desert," she said.

"Oral history was true of many cultures," Adrian pointed out before he went back to his restless pacing.

"You're right, of course, it was. But in the case of the ancient Egyptians, who were a highly civilized people for that time in history, these myths and legends were also painted onto tomb walls or carved into blocks of stone for temple and palace buildings. They were even incorporated into their jewelry." Christine gazed down at the scarab ring she was holding in her hand.

"Go on," Adrian said, a little urgently, she thought.

She continued. "Today we know the scenes depicted by the ancient Egyptians weren't realistic reflections of their history. They weren't meant to be taken literally. There were times of famine as well as years of plenty. Sometimes the Nile flooded too little and sometimes too much. There was death and there was destruction. Yet the battles are pictured only as victories, never as defeats. The pharaoh is shown only winning, never losing."

Adrian brought his teeth together. "And how would you answer my question as a woman?"

Christine tried to speak, but the breath caught in her throat. She was on the verge of tears again, she realized. "As a woman"—she had to pause and compose herself—"I would like to believe that love knows no boundaries, whether those boundaries be time or distance, or even death, itself."

Adrian stood stone still.

Christine went on. "As a woman I want to believe that love is forever, that love is eternal."

Adrian seemed to have stopped breathing.

She gave a self-conscious laugh. "I suppose that sounds very unrealistic and very romantic."

His eyes blazed like a hot blue fire. "Do you really believe that love knows no boundaries, Christine?"

She shivered. There was something almost frightening in the way Adrian was behaving. "Yes," she finally said in a whisper.

"I believe this as well," he said, lowering his voice to an intimate tone.

There was a long silence.

Christine stood and held out his gold cartouche ring. "Adrian," she prompted.

His eyes cleared. He seemed to come back from wherever he had gone. He glanced down at the ring, then up at her. "Haven't you wondered why I pressed my ring into your hand yesterday?"

"Of course I have." She just didn't know why. "You also said it was imperative that I come tonight."

"It is. There is something I must show you. Something I must tell you. Something I must try to explain to you," he said in a mesmerizing voice.

Christine glanced down at her watch. "It's getting late, Adrian. I really should be going back to the hotel."

"Not yet." He reached for her hand. "Come with me."

He led her out of the theater lounge, down a back hallway, through a maze of meeting rooms that were all a blur to her, and finally to another elevator marked PRIVATE. She'd never seen a hotel with so many private elevators.

"Where are we going?" she said

"We're going down."

"Down where?" Christine asked.

"To the wine cellar," Adrian answered.

TWENTY-FIVE

Christine no doubt thought him quite mad for dragging her down to his wine cellar at this hour of the night, Adrian realized as he entered the key code for the special storage area several levels below the parking garage of the Royal Palace.

Not that he could blame her.

He'd been questioning his own sanity more and more each day. Time suddenly seemed very precious to him, in short supply, limited. He felt driven to make every moment count, to miss no opportunity while he still had the chance.

A ridiculous notion, Adrian knew, when he was immortal and had all the time in the world. Yet there was a sense of urgency in everything he did. Logical or not, that's how it felt.

"I've read about your wine cellar," Christine volunteered. "It's supposed to be one of the finest in the country."

"It's one of the finest, if not *the* finest in the world," he said, without false modesty.

"I don't know much about wine," she admitted. "Although I like having a glass every now and then."

"You seemed to enjoy the Chateau d'Yquem the other evening," he pointed out.

She reddened. "It was very good."

Adrian almost chuckled. He'd forgotten how to laugh until Christine entered his life.

Very good, indeed. Chateau d'Yquem 1975 was considered an exquisite white wine. One of the best. Naturally, he only bought the best for his cellar.

The elevator came to a stop. The doors opened. Adrian stepped out and made certain Christine was right beside him. "It's this way," he said, indicating she should turn to the left.

"How many bottles of wine do you have in your cellar?" she asked, trying to make polite conversation.

Adrian shrugged. "At last count, somewhere between twenty-four and twenty-five thousand."

Gray eyes went wide. "Bottles?"

Adrian nodded.

Christine burst out with, "What does anyone do with twenty-four thousand bottles of wine?"

"Drink them."

That made her laugh. "It would take forever to drink that much wine," she observed.

Exactly, Adrian thought as he unlocked the solid wood door to the wine cellar.

The lights inside were programmed to come on automatically when he entered the tasting room. Another of the modern conveniences he enjoyed about living in this time and place.

Christine stepped inside and came to a halt. She took a moment to survey the finely crafted tables and chairs, sofas, and assorted other pieces of furniture. "This is a beautiful room."

"Thank you."

"But I don't see any bottles of wine," she said.

"This is the tasting room," Adrian explained. "The wine is stored in several larger areas off this one." He crossed the room and unlocked the next set of doors. More lights blinked on. There were wine racks and cases of wine as far as the eye could see.

"You weren't kidding," Christine said, duly impressed.

"About what?"

"Having enough wine stored down here to drink forever." She took several steps into the cellar. "Who comes down here?"·

"I do," Adrian replied.

She turned. "Don't you ever bring anyone else here?"

"A few select friends." Friends might not be precisely the right word, Adrian reflected. Friends were a luxury he had never permitted himself. At least not since he was a boy, and that was a very long time ago. "Mostly other wine connoisseurs. Sometimes a special guest of the hotel. Now and then, the odd politician."

"They're all a little odd, don't you find?" Christine said, without trying to be funny.

"We've also had a few successful fund-raisers here in the cellar," he said matter-of-factly.

"Putting your wine to work for a good cause," she proposed, strolling between the rows of bottles tilted at just the right angle for proper storage and aging.

"Something like that."

Christine finally turned and said to him, "As much as I'm enjoying the guided tour of your wine cellar, why did you bring me down here, Adrian?"

"There's something I want to show you," he said. "Something I've never shown anyone before."

Christine looked a little panic-stricken. "It doesn't have anything to do with all this wine, does it?"

"It has nothing to do with wine," he confirmed. "In fact, the wine is a red herring. It's what people are meant to see. They're so impressed by the millions upon millions of dollars worth of alcohol, the row after row of rare vintages of Burgundy and Bordeaux and champagne that they never suspect there might be something else down here."

"Now you're scaring me," Christine said, wrapping her arms around herself.

Adrian took a protective step toward her. "I'm not trying to frighten you. I'm trying to prepare you for what you're about to see."

This wasn't going exactly as he had planned, Adrian realized. But how else did he prepare Christine for what she was about to behold? How did you prepare anyone for that moment when their whole life was going to change?

Had he made a mistake in bringing her here tonight?

Or any night, for that matter?

Maybe she wasn't ready to learn the truth.

Adrian reached out for Christine's hand. "You once told me you weren't a gambler or a risk-taker."

She gave him a strange little smile. "I think that's changed, don't you?"

He stared hard into her eyes. "Are you brave?"

Christine seemed to understand it wasn't a frivolous question. "Yes, I am."

Adrian believed her. "Then come with me, Christine, and enter another time and place. Another world."

TWENTY-SIX

They approached the far corner of the fourth and final storage area in the wine cellar. More cases of wine were stacked against the back wall. This room was dusty, and unlike the rest of the cellar, it appeared to be unused and undisturbed. There were even a few cobwebs clinging to the shelving and wooden crates.

"These rooms are starting to all look alike," Christine ventured. Then she added, "I assume that's intentional."

"You assume correctly," Adrian said, reaching between several of the shelves and pressing some kind of mechanism or switch. Christine couldn't see exactly what he was doing, but suddenly a wall in front of them began to move.

Her initial reaction was to take a step back, but her curiosity drove her forward. "A false wall?"

Adrian shook his head. "A false door."

"A false door," she repeated, already beginning to examine the seams in the wood paneling.

A false door was usually a stone slab—although sometimes it was a wooden one—placed inside an Egyptian tomb or a mortuary palace. The door, or stele, was intended to serve as a link between the living and the dead. Offerings were often left in front of the false door for the person buried in the tomb. In fact, a figure of the deceased was traditionally carved into the stone, shown sitting at a table and ready to receive any offerings made. There were also inscriptions on the stele and the name of the person interred behind it.

But once the wall in Adrian's wine cellar had completely retracted like a pocket door, there was simply another wall: plain, bare, devoid of any ornamentation or decoration.

"It's just another wall," Christine said, stating the obvious, her disappointment showing.

"Not everything is as it seems," Adrian cautioned. Then he turned to her. "May I have the scarab ring?"

"Of course." Christine had slipped it onto her middle finger for safekeeping while they were still upstairs in the theater lounge. She removed the heavy gold ring and gave it to him.

Adrian positioned his hand on the second wall and a small, concealed compartment no larger than a man's thumb popped open. He took the ring, inserted it into the oddly shaped keyhole, and turned it three times counterclockwise. Then he removed the ring and placed it back on his own finger, where it belonged.

Christine realized she was holding her breath.

Nothing happened.

Her heart began to beat faster, in double time, then in triple. Her pulse was racing. She tried to swallow and found her mouth utterly dry; not a drop of saliva. Her head was hot, burning up like she was running a fever, but her hands were ice cold. She sensed something was about to change even before the second wall panel started to move on its track, seemingly in slow motion.

"Come on. Come on. Come on," Christine heard herself urging under her breath.

The panel opened to a width of four or five feet and then abruptly stopped.

A doorway was revealed.

But a doorway to where?

Or to *what*?

The door appeared to be old. Christine took a step closer. It was very old and covered with paintings and hieroglyphs. There was so much to examine that she didn't know where to look first.

"You may study the inscriptions in detail later," Adrian said as he reached around her and deactivated an alarm system that she hadn't even noticed.

"This place is better guarded than Fort Knox," she said, laughing nervously.

"It's worth more than Fort Knox," he said dryly.

Christine wasn't sure what to make of that comment. "I wonder what's behind door number one," she said, but her attempt at humor fell flat.

"It will speak for itself," Adrian assured her as he stepped closer and spoke in the ancient language: *"The door must open to the king and only to the king."*

"Voice-activated security."

He nodded as the stele silently glided open.

Christine's heart was suddenly in her throat. Somehow she knew that many of the answers she was seeking lay just beyond the threshold in front of her. The room was dark, cavernous, shadowed, but surely that was a glint of gold she had briefly glimpsed.

Adrian spoke again, this time in English. "Lights on."

One by one spotlights blinked on, beginning at the doorway and continuing around a huge room, a room seemingly swathed in black velvet, a room filled with treasure.

Christine froze. It was the kind of treasure you'd expect to find in a pharaoh's tomb, the kind Howard Carter had unearthed in November 1922 when he discovered Tutankhamen's virtually undisturbed tomb in the Valley of the Kings.

"It can't be real. It must be a joke."

Christine hadn't realized that she'd spoken out loud until Adrian answered her. "Believe me, it isn't a joke."

She flailed around for a reasonable explanation. "Reproductions, then? You have so many beautiful ones upstairs in your lobby. They're valuable in their own right, of course, but not priceless as a pharaonic treasure would be."

Adrian stood beside her, tall, broad-shouldered, regal. "They're not reproductions, Christine."

"But how . . . ?" She opened and closed her mouth. Time passed. She finally shook her head and whispered, "I must be dreaming. It wouldn't be the first time."

Adrian placed his hands on her shoulders and turned her toward him. "You aren't dreaming."

She was lost in a sea of blue. "I don't understand," she managed to say through lips that had gone numb.

Adrian sighed. "I know you don't."

"How can it be real?" She made up her mind. "It isn't real."

"It is real. It's as real as you or I," he stated.

"Did you steal the treasure?" Christine immediately rescinded her question. "How silly of me. How stupid of me to say that. Of course you didn't steal it. How could you? Where would you have stolen it from? There must be thousand of artifacts and hundreds of pounds of gold in this room. That's hardly something you can tuck into your pocket and walk out the door with."

"No, it isn't," he agreed.

"Besides, there hasn't been a discovery made of this magnitude since Tutankhamen's treasure. The whole world would know about it if there had been."

"Possibly," Adrian said evasively.

"Even a minor discovery couldn't be kept secret. Nothing's a secret in this day and age." She was finally starting to make sense again, Christine told herself. Of course, there was still no explanation for what she was seeing right before her eyes.

"I promise I'll answer all of your questions," Adrian said. "But, first, why don't you take some time and look around?"

"I believe I will," Christine said to him as she entered the treasure room.

The entrance was dominated by a pair of guardian figures, life-size, carved from wood, painted black with resin, and gilded with gold where there would have been an appropriate headdress, broad collar, pectorals, and armbands in life.

There was a statue of Anubis, lord of the west,

mounted on a shrine, and also gilded with gold. There was a row of jewel caskets on Christine's left and countless shelves of alabaster jars that no doubt contained unguents, oils, food, even wine at some point. Whether they still did was questionable.

There was a beautifully carved and gilded bed, a chair fit for a king and encrusted with semi-precious gemstones, and various other pieces of ornate furniture, including several ritual couches.

There were gold statues of animals and birds. An elegant ebony game box rested on its four-legged stand. There were ivory musical instruments and silver trumpets, dozens of ceremonial daggers, fighting sticks, and boomerangs.

The sheer volume and variety of jewelry was mind-boggling, Christine judged as she neared the end of the first row and began to make her way back toward the door.

Adrian was strolling majestically toward her.

"Now I understand how Howard Carter must have felt when he beheld Tutankhamen's treasure for the first time," she said in a voice choked with emotion.

"I doubt if Tutankhamen's tomb was this well-lighted or displayed on black velvet," Adrian said with a sardonic smile.

Christine made a wide, sweeping gesture with her hand. "It's all real, isn't it?"

But she already knew in her heart of hearts it was.

Adrian stopped in front of her and gazed down into her upturned face. "You sense it is real, don't you?"

She nodded. "I've always been able to detect the real from the fake." She shrugged her shoulders. "Another one of my odd and inexplicable talents as an Egyptologist."

"Or perhaps your special feminine intuition?"

"Perhaps," Christine said with a sigh.

"You think you know whose burial treasure this is, too, don't you?" Adrian went on to say.

How could she not know? Merneptah Seti's name was inscribed on everything from the furniture to the golden shrines, from dozens of pieces of precious jewelry to the ceremonial daggers.

"Where did you find the ancient pharaoh's treasure?" Christine wanted to know, *needed* to know. And how had Adrian King succeeded where her grandfather and his grandfather before him had failed?

"This isn't an ancient pharaoh's treasure," Adrian boldly declared.

"Of course it is," Christine said, not understanding why he would say something so outrageous.

"It isn't. It's *my* treasure," Adrian insisted.

TWENTY-SEVEN

Christiane was looking at him like he was insane. "I am not crazy and I am not delusional," Adrian proclaimed, his voice echoing throughout the wine cellar, bouncing off the walls, and coming back on them like a cacophony of trumpets.

A fierce battle was raging within him. It was far from the first such battle, he acknowledged to himself. There was always an internal struggle going on between his rational mind and his emotions, between the man and the beast.

By all the mighty gods, he didn't have to explain himself to anyone! He was Adrian King. He was *the* king.

Christine is your destiny, a small voice said inside his head.

If he didn't tell her who he was, if he refused to tell

her how he came to possess Merneptah Seti's treasure, she would leave him. Where would he be then?

What would he become without her?

Something in his heart and soul whispered that he would be lost forever.

"You're not accustomed to explaining yourself to anyone, especially to a woman, are you?" Christine said with her usual uncanny ability to read his mind.

Adrian gritted through his teeth, "No, I'm not."

"Well, you don't have to explain anything to me," she said, making herself perfectly clear.

"I must, or I know you will leave." It wasn't a question; it was a statement.

Christine didn't deny it.

Adrian hadn't expected her to.

"I don't know where to begin," he said in preamble.

"Then I won't say something like 'begin at the beginning.' " Christine wetted her lips. She appeared to be relatively calm and collected despite what must seem like an outrageous claim on his part. He would explain everything, of course, in due time. "Why don't you start with how you managed to move this huge amount of treasure from Egypt, from the Valley of the Kings, to a vault in the basement of your hotel?" she said.

He could do that.

"It wasn't as difficult as you might think," Adrian said, feeling his shoulders relax a little.

"Difficult? I think it's impossible," Christine interjected.

He shook his head from side to side. "Not if you know the right people."

She appeared curious. "And who would the right people be in this case?"

Adrian decided to skim over some of the details. After all, there was no reason to name names. Discretion had been absolutely essential to the success of many of his ventures. "There are those who are willing to be bribed. Those who turn their heads the other way for a moment. Those who help disguise a genuine antiquity within an obvious fake in order to pass through Customs. Those who have sworn their allegiance and their very lives to me long, long ago."

Christine shivered.

Adrian expressed his concern. "Are you cold?"

She shook her head.

"The rest was relatively easy," Adrian said, continuing with his recounting of the events. "I was building this hotel. What was one more room in a vast warren of rooms designated as a wine cellar? I was having cases of wine shipped in on a regular schedule. What were a few more boxes? There were genuine and documented antiquities arriving on a weekly basis, craftsmen were coming from all over the world to work on and create perfect reproductions of famous statues, furniture, even jewelry."

"So the genuine articles were brought in under the radar," Christine surmised, her hand going to her mouth in astonishment.

Adrian nodded. "Once everything was completed, once the proper controls and the security measures were in place, I made certain that the only one who knew all of the controls and all of the security measures was myself."

"You're the only one who comes down here to the treasure room," Christine concluded.

"I am the only one." Then Adrian added, "Until tonight."

"You're very trusting," she said, after a minute.

"I assure you, just the contrary is true. I trust no one but myself," he stated.

Christine gazed up into his face. "What about Rahotep?"

"Rahotep has sworn to serve and protect me. I trust him to do as he has sworn."

"He would give his life for you?"

"Yes."

"And what of me?" Christine took a deep breath and held it in her lungs before slowly exhaling. "Why have you chosen to share a secret of this magnitude with me?" He knew she still thought his claim was insane.

Adrian reached down and placed his hand on the side of her face, cradling her chin. "Because I trust you implicitly, Christine."

"So it would seem that you do trust someone besides yourself," she pointed out to him.

"Yes, I suppose I do." She was right, of course. There might not be many within his most intimate and trusting circle, but there was Rahotep and now there was Christine.

"And I trust you," she said, and her words rang true.

"Even though there are some things that you don't know about me," Adrian said very seriously.

Christine laughed. It was a dark and ironic laugh, not her usual delighted laugh at all. "*Some* things? That's the understatement of the century. There are a million things about you that I don't know."

Adrian knew what was uppermost in her mind. His declaration that this was *his* treasure. He frowned. "What would you like to know?"

"Everything," she shot back. "But I suppose that would take a lifetime or longer." She went on. "You play your cards very close to your chest, Mister King."

"Some of us have to."

"Yes, we do," she murmured, almost as if she were speaking to herself.

"In order to survive," Adrian finished.

Christine stared straight into his eyes. "It was a matter of life and death for you, wasn't it?"

"Yes." He paused and considered, then spoke. "What was it for you?"

Her eyes, eyes that were intelligent, but eyes that had always been wary, always been guarded; eyes that concealed far more than they revealed, suddenly cleared. "For me, it was a matter of sanity or insanity," she said.

"That can be a kind of life and death, too," Adrian purposed thoughtfully.

"I suppose it can be in a way," Christine said, thinking out loud. "I've kept so many secrets for so many years, in order that others wouldn't judge me, wouldn't think me insane, and put me under a doctor's care and fill me with pills." She shivered and wrapped her arms around herself. "Or lock me away somewhere."

"Why would anyone question your sanity?" Adrian asked, dark brows furrowing.

Christine appeared to make up her mind. "I will share one of my secrets with you since you have shared one of yours with me," she said, sounding resolved.

Adrian was surprised by her offer. It had been a very

long time since someone had chosen to share a secret with him. People had secrets, of course. But he was always able to discern them without their knowledge and without their permission. "I am honored," he said, and realized that he meant it.

Christine seemed to steel herself for what she was about to say. "I have dreams."

Adrian blinked several times in rapid succession. He didn't understand. "We all have dreams."

Christine's skin went very pale. The veins on the backs of her hands, in the hollow of her throat, and on the side of her neck appeared to be blue, as blue as the Blue Nile, vivid blue on white alabaster flesh. She moistened her lips. "I have dreams while I'm sleeping, and I have what I call 'waking' dreams."

"You mean visions?"

"I suppose you could call them visions." A deep sigh escaped her. "I've had them since I was a child. As a matter of fact, for as long as I can remember."

"I see." But Adrian wasn't sure that he did. "What do you see in these 'waking' dreams?"

She hesitated for a moment. "Places I've never been to. People I've never met. Things I've never done."

"Dreams of the future?"

"I'm not certain."

"Dreams of the past?"

She nodded. "Yes, dreams of the past." She went on to explain further. "Dreams of the ancient past. Often of Egypt in the time of the pharaohs."

Adrian did not smile, although he realized he was tempted to. He did not want to make light of Christine's confession or her secret. He would not wish to hurt her feelings.

"Is it surprising that you would dream of the Black Land when your grandfather and his grandfather before him spent much of their lives in Egypt, studying, researching, digging in the Valley of the Kings for these pharaohs?" he said.

"I suppose not." But she didn't sound convinced.

"Didn't you tell me that your grandfather often returned from one of his journeys and told you bedtime stories, filling your heart and mind with tales of ancient kings?"

"Yes, he did."

"Well . . ." Adrian said and shrugged.

"The thing is, I had a 'waking' dream the night I walked into your hotel, before we had even met each other."

He stood very still.

Christine lowered her eyes. When she looked up again, there was a tear poised on the edge of an eyelash. Just one. But it affected Adrian deeply, more than countless tears from anyone else. "And yet the person I saw in my waking dream," she admitted, "was you."

TWENTY-EIGHT

"I'm not crazy and I'm not delusional," Christine said, repeating the same words Adrian had used earlier.

He gave a decisive nod of his head. "I believe you are the most sane person I've ever met."

"Thank you," she said, knowing she sounded pleased. She *was* pleased.

"How long have you been dreaming about me?" Adrian asked, his eyes glinting curiously.

This was no time for coyness, Christine thought. "All of my life. Of course, in the beginning they were a child's dreams filled with visions of a mighty warrior and the mysterious figure of the Sphinx and the Great Pyramids of Giza."

"All children are intrigued by the Sphinx and the

Great Pyramids," Adrian commented. "I, too, dreamed of these things as a boy."

"It wasn't until I was older, until I was a young woman, in fact, that my dreams changed," she said.

Adrian spoke interrogatively. "Changed in what way?"

Christine was candid. "I began to see the man in my dreams in a romantic light. But he was always featureless. Or I should say, I never actually saw his face. Still, I knew if I ran into him I would definitely recognize him."

"And did you?" Adrian asked.

"Yes."

"When was this?"

"It was that first night here at the Royal Palace. I'd wandered down a corridor and stopped for a moment by the lotus pool. I dipped my fingers into the water and suddenly I was having one of my 'waking' dreams, one of my visions, as you call them. But with one big difference: This time I clearly saw the man's face."

"And?" Adrian urged.

"I heard footsteps behind me. I turned around and there was the man of my dreams . . . there you were."

Adrian was following her words with the closest attention. "I've had dreams about you, as well."

"You have? For how long?" Christine said, after the briefest of pauses.

Adrian frowned as he folded his arms across his chest. "For a long time."

She was hoping for a more precise answer. "Exactly how long is a long time?"

The air suddenly shifted around them, and there was the scent of spice in Christine's nostrils. She could smell the desert. She could hear the Nile running and the boatmen singing, chanting in the ancient tongue, as they dipped their oars into the River of Life. She could see the stars in the heavens above, and the outline of a Great Pyramid against the night sky.

"I have been dreaming of you for thousands of years," Adrian said simply, poetically.

"How?" That wasn't the question she thought she was going to ask him.

And it wasn't the question he answered. "I haven't always gone by the name of Adrian King. That is a name I gave myself thirty years ago," he said.

She took a nervous breath. "Why?"

His mouth went hard. "Because I could not use the name I was given at birth."

"I've been wondering who you really are since we met," Christine admitted.

Adrian was silent for a moment, evidently mulling it over. "I want to tell you the truth, but the truth is—"

"Always the truth," she finished for him.

His face clouded. "Not everyone sees the truth. Not everyone believes the truth when they hear it."

"I will."

Christine noticed a subtle change in Adrian's posture when he said, "You told me tonight after we left the the-ater that the love story in the *The Book of the Dead* brought you to tears."

"It did," she confirmed, trying to keep the quiver out of her voice. "I was so moved I couldn't speak. I couldn't breathe. I was afraid if I opened my mouth, every emotion in my body would come pouring out. It's the reason I couldn't eat or drink after the show."

Adrian seemed pleased with her response. "The story of the ancient pharaoh and the woman he sees in his dreams is true," he stated.

"It is?" After a pause Christine went on. "It isn't one I've ever heard before, but I doubt if anybody is acquainted with every story, legend, or myth about ancient Egypt."

"Not even an expert like yourself?"

She gave a self-deprecating little laugh. "Not even an expert like myself." Then she recalled a bedtime talk she'd had many years ago with Grandpapa. "I've just remembered something," she said to Adrian.

"What?"

"It's a conversation I had with my grandfather the night he gave me the ancient papyrus."

Adrian drew a breath and spoke very deliberately. "Tell me more about this conversation."

She swallowed before going on, "Even at the age of nine I knew immediately what was written on the sheet of papyrus. I knew it was a recipe for a scented oil and I knew who had written it."

Dark eyes engaged hers. "Who wrote it?"

"King Merneptah Seti." She hurried on. "I remember telling my grandfather that the king had created the perfume for the woman who came to him in his dreams, the woman he called 'his secret.' "

Adrian stiffened visibly. "How did you know this?"

Christine frowned. "I don't know. But I do know it was unusual because a king would normally have his dreams interpreted by his priests. For whatever reason Seti decided to keep this dream a secret from them, from everyone." She gave her head an emphatic shake.

"I even blurted out that I thought the pharaoh was in love with the woman who came to him in his dreams."

"And what did your grandfather say to that?"

"He laughed and asked how a child could know anything of such love." Christine sighed heavily. "At the time I couldn't explain it to myself, let alone to him. It wasn't as if I understood the intimate details of love between a man and a woman, but even a child can understand longing, can understood loneliness."

"You were a most unusual child," Adrian observed.

"I was certainly always aware that I was different," she said a little too softly.

"Finish your story about that night," came the reminder.

Christine cleared her throat and continued. "I also couldn't explain how I knew what the perfumed oil smelled like just by reading the list of ingredients, but I did. And I remember saying to my grandfather that it must have been very lonely to be a king."

"Did he agree with you?"

"Yes. Then he said he was getting old and time was running out for him. That made me feel like crying because I couldn't bear the thought of losing the one person who shared my passion for ancient Kemet, the one person who might understand what my dreams meant. Grandpapa even admitted to me that he was afraid he would never find Seti. That's when I made him a promise."

"What was your promise?"

She'd never told anyone else until now. "I promised my grandfather that one day I would find his king for him."

"Then what happened?"

"Then I came back from that memory to the present. I was standing by the fountain and staring at you."

Adrian held up his hands, examining the palms, then slowly lowered his arms. "What if I were to tell you that you've kept your promise to Lawrence Day?"

Christine found herself in the grip of an odd feeling of disquiet. "I don't understand."

He put a hand—just a finger or two—against her lips. "My people used to believe that dreams had power."

Her pulse beat double. "Used to?"

"Most of my people vanished long ago," he told her feelingly.

Her voice was reed thin. "Where did they go?"

Adrian seemed to weigh his answer before he said to her, "Into legend."

Christine stared searchingly at him. "Who are you really?"

"I will tell you and I will show you," Adrian replied, taking her hand and guiding her into a special alcove inside the treasure room.

Christine hadn't noticed the niche before. There had been so much to look at, so much to see, so much to comprehend that had truly been incomprehensible, that it was impossible to take it all in.

Adrian stopped before a special display case. It contained two objects. One was a beautiful gold mask, not unlike the fabled gold mask of Tutankhamen. Yet somehow, the features on this mask seemed familiar.

Christine leaned over and studied the carved face in detail. Portrait masks weren't meant to be literal depic-

tions of the deceased, but this one seemed far less ideal-
istic and far more realistic than most. And she was getting that funny feeling again; the one that told her to go
with her gut, and not her head.

She straightened and turned to the man standing beside her. "Adrian, it looks like you," she said.

"It *is* me," he said simply. He pointed to a piece of
papyrus in the case beside the mask.

Christine leaned over again and discovered it was a
poem. She read it several times to herself and then the
final lines aloud in the ancient language, " 'Thou art favored by the gods. They call thee by name. And when
they see thee come it is said: The Beautiful One
comes.' " She straightened.

Adrian's blue eyes burned into hers, imprinting
themselves on her very heart and soul. "I am the man
who dreamed long ago of a woman," he said. "I wrote
poetry in her honor. I created a perfumed oil for her. For
centuries she existed only in my dreams. Then one night
not so long ago I smelled the ancient perfume for the
first time in more than three millennia. I followed the
scent and I found her. I found you, Christine."

Her heart thrummed violently. "When . . . when was
this mask created?"

"In the year you now refer to as 1192 B.C.E."

She closed her eyes and tried to think. "And when
was the poem written?"

Adrian's sonorous voice moved along her nerve endings, playing them like violin strings that were strung
too tightly and which might snap at any moment. "A
few years before that." Then he asked, "Did you look at
the woman's face at the bottom of the poem?"

Christine opened her eyes and gazed down at the piece of papyrus. There was no mistaking the image sketched by his ancient hand. "It looks like me," she said through lips gone numb.

"It *is* you, Christine."

Her rational mind kept telling her it was some kind of crazy coincidence, but her heart—well, her heart saw the truth. She looked up at the man standing at her side and she knew he had once been a fierce warrior, a wise leader of his people, a great king. It was written on his face, and evident in his bearing, even in his stature. Indeed, this man was still a king. "I know who you are," she said at last.

"Yes, you do," he said.

Christine felt the words trembling on her tongue. "You are Merneptah Seti."

TWENTY-NINE

Later that night as they lay side by side in his bed in the master suite, Adrian turned and gazed intently into Christine's eyes. Then, in slow motion, he brought his lips to within a fraction of an inch of hers.

"I don't want to think anymore," she murmured. "I don't want to talk anymore. I don't want to try to make sense of things that make no sense. I simply want to *feel*."

Adrian granted her wish. He whispered to her in the ancient language, "I am thirsty."

"Then drink," Christine urged as he took her mouth.

It was as a kiss should be and rarely was. It was hot and cold. It drove him away and beckoned him closer. It captured and held him, and yet it set him free. It satisfied him and it made him yearn hungrily, desperately, crazily for more.

It was only a kiss, Adrian thought. It was nothing; it was everything.

Christine's mouth tasted of Christine and only Christine. That's the only way he knew how to describe her taste, her scent, the texture of her mouth. It was sweet and bitter, spicy, alluring, intoxicating, addictive, inexplicably so.

Then he felt his breathing change as he pressed his mouth to her breast, drew her nipple between his teeth and nipped and licked and sucked even as he eased his finger lower, lower still, then between the damp chestnut-brown curls until he slipped his finger inside her.

He wetted his hand with her body's moisture. He gently flicked her clitoris several times; she jerked with each arousing touch. He dipped into her again a little farther this time. She groaned her need out loud, her desire for more, and so he slipped his finger in all the way.

"I love to feel you, your hands, on me, inside me," Christine confessed to him in a whisper. That was the moment he plunged in ever deeper and deeper, and even followed, after a moment, with a second finger.

She moaned aloud and instinctively lifted her hips off the bed, driving her breast deeper into his mouth, and causing his finger to thrust even farther into her body. He could feel the tiny convulsions begin inside her, knew the moment when her heart seemed to cease its beating, sensed herself nearing the brink, and called out his name in that instant before she was catapulted over the edge.

Then he withdrew his hand, and he could feel her quiver when he took his first taste of her with his tongue, and the gasp of astonishment as he took it a step further and nibbled on the sensitive nub with just the serrated edges of his teeth. And when he finally decided the time had come, he took a long and hearty drink of the sweet wine she offered.

"Adrian. Adrian. Adrian." He heard his name become a litany on her lips.

Some time later, Christine pushed herself up onto her elbows and gazed down into his face. Her hair fell in a wild tumble around her shoulders. She impatiently pushed at its unmanageable mass, trying to secure it behind her ears, but several errant strands escaped, and brushed along his bare skin even as she dragged her mouth from one side of his chest to the other and back again.

She seemed to savor his flesh as if she found his taste very much to her liking. She nipped at him with the sharp little edges of her teeth, and it was pleasure that was almost pain, and the near pain that was, indeed, pleasure. She nibbled and feasted and devoured him as though she were half-starved and he could somehow satisfy the terrible hunger inside of her.

He heard a moan of sexual arousal. It came from Christine, but it echoed again and again inside him.

With her tongue she traced the pattern of soft, dark hair that encircled each male nipple, and then followed the narrow path it took down the center of his chest. She drew a damp ring around the indentation of his navel and his muscles clenched. She licked her way lower, finding him, wetting him with her tongue, tasting him, testing him, then taking him into her mouth and threatening to swallow him whole.

She raised her head only long enough to murmur in a

low, husky contralto unlike her usual voice: "I love the way you feel. I love the way you taste."

Then Adrian nudged her onto her back, eased himself between her legs, looked down into her eyes, and thrust into her.

"Stay with me, Christine," he commanded as he drove stronger, harder, deeper. Then, with a triumphant shout, he exploded inside her.

And as their bodies finally joined completely, the past and the present became one.

THIRTY

Adrian came out of a dead sleep.

He shot straight up in bed.

His heart was banging against his ribs.

He was breathing hard.

He was covered with sweat.

The room was dark.

Pitch-black.

The stink was overpowering; it filled his nostrils, his lungs, his mind. Not just the trace he'd smelled once before. No, this was the overwhelming, all-consuming stench of pure . . . *evil*.

THIRTY-ONE

Candy picked up the phone on the first ring. She assumed it was Jason. It'd better be Jason. "Where the hell are you?" she demanded to know in a petulant tone, snapping her gum.

A man's voice, deep and compelling, cultured, inquired politely, "May I please speak with Miss Candy Adams?"

Candy spit her gum out into the butt-filled ashtray on the bedside table. She sat up straighter, quit slouching, hitched up the bra strap that kept slipping off her left shoulder and down her arm, and said, "Sorry about that. This is her."

Or was it, This is *she*? Candy could never remember. "This is your employer, Mister Smith."

Candy almost laughed right in his ear. She was willing to bet Smith wasn't his real name. She almost said: *Are you sure this isn't Mister Jones?* But she caught herself in the nick of time. Their employer might not have a sense of humor. He might think she was being a wiseass and hold it against her. "Hello, Mister Smith."

"Is Jason Stanford-White there?" the mellifluous voice inquired. The guy sure had a nice way of talking.

"I'm sorry, Mister Smith, he isn't. Jason had to step out for a few minutes."

What a dumb time for Jason to decide to make a beer and cigarette run, Candy thought, disgusted. But then Jason was an idiot every day of the week and twice on Sundays, as her grandma used to say about men in general. How long did it take to run down to the corner store for a six-pack and some cigs? Ten minutes. Fifteen, tops.

Candy glanced at the clock bolted to the top of the wood veneer dresser. Jason had already been gone for several hours. The jerk was probably somewhere wasting the small advance Mr. Smith had paid them at the beginning of this job. Well, $2,000 wasn't small potatoes, but it was nothing compared to what they had been promised once the job was finished.

Frankly, Candy realized, she was a little vague on exactly what else they had to do to earn the remainder of their money: The promised twenty-five thou each.

"It's of no importance if Jason isn't there," said the velvety voice on the other end of the phone line. "You're the one I want to speak with, anyway, Miss Adams."

"I am?" That put a ridiculously pleased expression on her face. Kind of made her day, in fact.

"Yes, you are. By the way, how did you like wearing

the evening gown and the gemstone jewelry the night you were sent to the Royal Palace?"

"Are you kidding?" Candy snorted. Then remembered she was supposed to be playing the lady. "I was born to wear designer clothes and expensive jewelry."

"I agree," said Mr. Smith. "Would you like to do it on a more permanent basis?"

Candy took in a lungful of air. She felt a little giddy. Or maybe it was plain old dizziness since she hadn't eaten much today: only a handful of chips and half a can of cola that had lost its fizz. It was a full five seconds before she could speak. "I sure would." Then her common sense—what little she had—kicked in. "What would I have to do? I mean, it wouldn't be nothing illegal or anything, would it?"

"Of course, not," came the assurance.

"You know, we were kicked out of the Royal Palace that night. The security guards claimed Jason was counting cards or something. I think it's because he was winning too much money." Candy swallowed hard. "We didn't do anything wrong."

"No, you didn't, Miss Adams. It's not illegal to count cards, but since it puts the casinos at a disadvantage the gaming commission and the law in Nevada err on the side of the gambling establishments. A casino is permitted to ask a guest to leave if or when card counting is suspected. They don't even have to prove it. In fact, they can ask anyone to leave at any time. They don't have to give a reason."

"That doesn't seem fair," she said, pouting.

"No, it doesn't." The gentleman cleared his throat and inquired, "Would you be interested in making an additional ten thousand on your own tonight?"

She wasn't born yesterday, Candy reminded herself, although she kept her real age a closely guarded secret. "It depends on what I have to do for it, sir." She added the "sir" because she thought it sounded more professional and respectful.

"All you have to do is dress in the evening gown I gave you, do your hair and nails—you know, look your best—and visit several of the large downtown casinos, placing a number of bets here and there on the roulette wheels."

Candy gulped. "Does it matter if I win or lose? I'm not much of a gambler."

"It doesn't matter at all. I'm more interested in having you seen. I know for a fact that a number of bigwig movie and TV producers are in town. If you catch the right one's eye, there may even some bit parts on primetime or cameo roles in movies."

Candy was thrilled. "I've always wanted to break into show biz. This could be my big chance."

"It certainly could."

Then she frowned. "What do you get out of this arrangement, Mister Smith?" He must want something. Everybody wanted something.

"If I think you have enough talent to make it in Tinsel Town, I'll act as your agent. I'll help you get your career off the ground."

Candy forgot and snapped her gum again.

Mr. Smith went on to explain the particulars. "Within the next half hour an envelope will be slipped under the door of your motel room. Inside you will find the list of casinos you are to visit this evening and the cash you'll need for gambling."

"What happens if I lose all the money?"

"Then you can consider your job done and you may return to your motel room."

"That's all I have to do," she repeated, just to make certain she understood.

"That's all you have to do," the kind, masculine voice on the other end of the phone told her.

Candy was a little hesitant to ask, but no guts, no glory as they said. "When do I get my ten thousand?"

"It will be in a plain brown envelope waiting for you at the motel manager's desk tomorrow morning. That way you can slip out and pick it up when Jason isn't around."

"What Jason doesn't know won't hurt him," she said.

Mr. Smith laughed. It was a nice laugh. She wished more men sounded like that when they laughed. "You're absolutely right, Miss Adams. What Jason doesn't know, won't hurt him."

THIRTY-TWO

The female had made a most unsatisfying meal, Seth ruminated as he reached into the inner pocket of his tuxedo jacket and withdrew a gold toothpick with a diamond tip.

Miss Candy Adams, as she called herself, had been a disappointment to him. Not that he had believed for a minute that was her real name, any more than he'd believed that she had been naturally endowed with such oversized assets. He had been able to smell the silicone in her breasts even before he bit into them.

Yes, dear, sweet, naive, and rather stupid Candy had been just a little too quick to do as he'd asked, a little too eager to please her "employer," a little too greedy for what he could offer her. He loved playing elaborate games, loved the challenge of creating and executing them. It had been his experience that the enticement of jewels and money bedazzled most women. But the vague lure of a career in "show biz" had been enough to tempt Candy.

She had been a fool.

Now she was dead.

Seth looked up at the man watching him from across the room. His eyes were huge, frightened.

"Frightened isn't quite the correct word though, is it, Jason?" Seth said aloud as he approached his next victim, flicking the dagger in his hand as if it were a child's toy.

Jason was gagging, vomiting, choking behind the masking tape covering his mouth.

Seth made a sound of supreme disdain. All men were *not* created equal. This lowly human being didn't deserve to breathe the same air that he breathed, and before long he wouldn't.

Of course, you are not merely a man, Seth said to himself. *You are more—so much more—than a man. You are a god. You are immortal. You are invincible.*

He flicked the point of the dagger at Jason's throat, pricked the skin ever so slightly, and then watched as a small stream of blood appeared and began to flow down the man's neck.

Jason's fright quickly became terror.

"That's better," Seth said in a soft and seductive tone.

The thrill wasn't merely to drink the humans' blood, to drain them dry until they were no more than an empty shell. *Au contraire,* the thrill was draining the emotions from their bodies as they gave up their life force to him.

Seth found he was in the mood for a little conversation. "I'm not the first warrior to drink his enemy's blood, you know."

Jason began to twist his body, to struggle against the ropes that bound him.

"You know you're wasting your time and energy, Jason, my boy," Seth lectured in a tone that had often been used in the past by schoolmasters chiding their young charges. "I've made very sure the ropes are thick enough and secure enough that even a superman couldn't free himself of them." Then he smiled and was tempted to brag just a smidgen. "Well, *I* could free myself, of course. But then you're not me, are you?"

Eyes as large as saucers, Jason shook his head. Seth assumed it was in agreement.

"As I was saying before I was so rudely interrupted by your feeble attempts to free yourself, I'm not the first to drink my enemy's blood. As a matter of fact, it was once common in many warrior cultures. Look up the history of the Mayans or the Aztecs, if you don't believe me." Then Seth slapped the dagger against his thigh, glanced down, realized he had inadvertently transferred a streak of blood from the dagger to his dress trousers, and made a *tsk-tsk* sound of complaint. "Now look what you made me do."

He raised the bloody dagger to his lips and licked it clean.

Seth slowly strolled toward Jason Stanford-White, anticipated and then savored the expression of terror on his victim's face as it became sheer horror.

Seth felt the bloodlust flooding his veins, the acid bubbling up in his throat, his incisors growing, extending, and he knew that his razor-sharp teeth were far more lethal than the puny dagger he held in his grasp.

His diction was hampered by his fangs, but he made an extra effort to be understood when he said to the human, "I'm not the first to drink his enemy's blood or the first to eat his enemy's heart."

THIRTY-THREE

Something was wrong.

Adrian could smell it. The foul odor filled his nostrils. It burned his throat raw as if he had inhaled acrid smoke. It hit him like a fist to his solar plexus. It twisted his guts into a *cartonnage* knot. It made his eyes see the world in shades of red and scarlet.

His senses were overwhelmed, swamped, flooded; the stink of rage was on the verge of breaking through the protective shield that kept him in control, kept him sane.

And yet you draw ever closer to insanity, to madness, to that terrible and damning temptation with each passing day, Adrian thought morosely as he stood on the rooftop terrace of the Royal Palace and gazed out at the neon lights of Sin City below him.

The unmistakable sensation of complete and utter wrongness hit him again, harder this time, like a mortal blow to the heart. For a minute or two he couldn't breathe, wasn't sure he could keep his balance or stay upright on his feet.

Something was changing.

Growing.

Distorting.

Distending.

His mouth contorted. His jaw jutted forward. His lips formed a permanent leer. His gums swelled, bled. His teeth lengthened, sharpened, dripped with a solution that boiled his flesh. He suddenly felt deformed, disfigured, perverted.

He knew in his soul that evil was present.

What if the evil was him?

Adrian closed his eyes and sought that place of solace deep within himself, the place where he still retained some semblance of calm, the place where he kept his thoughts and dreams and hopes—and, yes, his love for Christine—alive.

She is your salvation.

No! a voice—his voice—screamed inside his brain. There was no salvation for him, for any of those who had awakened. There was always a price to be paid for eternal existence, and no one was exempt from paying that price.

Not even him.

Not even a king.

Adrian knew what his future held: He would become the Demon, the Monster, an Eater of Blood and a Breaker of Bones.

A Vampire.

But not now and not tonight. For tonight he could and *would* still maintain control.

His mouth and jaw returned to their former, normal state. He wiped the drops of blood from his lips with the back of his hand. His teeth retracted into his gums. His skin felt bruised, burned, but nothing more. He was himself again.

But for how long?

He must warn Christine of the danger. He must somehow convince her that she had to leave for her own sake and her own safety. Not just leave him, but leave Las Vegas, and get as far away as possible from anyone and anything to do with him.

"How will you persuade her to go?" Adrian asked aloud, laughing darkly, sardonically at his own self-interests and his own selfish desires that had brought this dilemma down upon him . . . and upon her. "What can you say that will drive her away now that you have confided your secrets to her?"

Not all of his secrets, of course. Even Christine didn't know all there was to know about him.

He would find the words.

He had to find them.

"I thought I'd find you out here on the terrace," came the most beautiful voice he had ever heard. "I wasn't sure what wine you preferred tonight, so I chose one myself. I've been studying up on fine wines, you know?"

Adrian turned to Christine and managed a semblance of a smile. "And what have you chosen for us?"

She handed him one of the two wineglasses she was carrying. "Why don't you tell me?"

Adrian brought the crystal glass up to his nose and breathed in. He could tell instantly what the wine would taste like on his tongue, how it would feel when he held it in his mouth and allowed it to permeate his senses.

He knew with a single whiff where the grape had been grown, what kind of climate the region had known that year, what the soil had been enriched with, what trees had grown nearby, and what the surrounding countryside had been like.

The French called it *terroir*.

It was one of the reasons he had always enjoyed wine: He could taste it, smell it, savor its nuances. Through the grapes he could experience the sun and the rain that had fallen on the vineyard. He could feel the hands that had picked the grapes, hear the voices, sense the laughter and tears of those who had worked in the field.

Wine came to him in flavors and colors and sounds. Wine made him remember. And, if he were lucky, it made him forget. At least for a small space of time.

Adrian took a drink of the red wine and held it on the roof of his mouth for a moment or two. Its fragrance filled him. Then he swallowed and said to Christine, "An excellent choice."

"Thank you," she said, smiling. "And . . . ?"

"It's Burgundy. Chambertin Clos de Bèze." There was never any mistaking its inimitable taste. "It was Napoleon's personal favorite, by the way."

Christine opened and closed her mouth in astonishment. "You cheated. You must have seen the label on the bottle." Then she burst out laughing and admitted, "Although I don't think even you can see through walls."

Adrian took another sip, although he already knew the year, and said, "1988."

Christine planted one hand on her hip. "How in the world did you know that?"

"You must remember I've been drinking wine for a little longer than you have."

Her mouth turned up at the corners. "That's true."

Adrian took a deep breath. It was time. He couldn't put it off any longer or they just might run out of time. "You've chosen an excellent wine for our farewell toast."

Christine's glass paused in midair. "Farewell toast?" She raised her eyes to his. "Are you going somewhere?"

He did not move. "No."

She looked briefly disconcerted. She reached down and smoothed the skirt of her dress: The silky material was a shade of soft gray that perfectly matched the color of her eyes, Adrian realized.

"I don't understand," she said at last.

"I know you don't." The wine had suddenly lost its flavor and its pleasure for him.

A terrible silence descended on the terrace.

Christine turned and placed her wineglass on the table behind them. "What are you saying, Adrian?"

"I'm saying that it's time for you to go," he said, determined to maintain control of the situation.

Christine was a stubborn woman. She was a worthy challenge, as he had rightly judged that first night when they met by the lotus pool. She was a consort fit for a king.

She put her shoulders back and said to him, without quarter, "Go where?"

"Chicago," he replied.

She didn't hesitate. "Why?"

Adrian gave her an imposing look. He was not used to having his instructions questioned. "Because that is where you live and work," he pointed out as if he were simply being reasonable.

"And when did you make this decision, Mister King?" The emphasis was on the word *Mister*.

"This evening."

She was tenacious. "When this evening?"

His face hardened. He almost didn't answer her. "A few minutes ago."

Her lips folded in that soft obstinate line he was becoming familiar with. "What happened a few minutes ago?"

Now it was Adrian's turn to admit, "I don't understand."

"Something has happened," Christine stated. "Something that you're not telling me."

"There are things that happen that I will not tell you or that I choose not to tell you," he said, raising his voice a tone or two from its usual deep baritone.

"Secrets," she said simply.

Adrian's brow furrowed. "Secrets?"

Christine reached out and took his hand in hers. Her touch was warm. His flesh was cold. The welcomed heat began to flow from her body into his. "We both have so many secrets. Secrets we've never shared with anyone. Secrets we've only shared with each other. Inconsequential secrets. Intimate secrets. Significant secrets. We'll never have time to tell each other all of them. But some secrets should not be kept secret, Adrian." She gazed long into his eyes. "I was your secret for three thousand years. Please tell me what's wrong."

"You must go because you can't stay."

"Why?"

"I can't tell you."

"You can. You must."

He narrowed his eyes. "You must go because you are in danger."

Christine appeared bewildered. "From what?"

There was a distinct chill in the air.

Adrian's warning was ominous. "Not what. Who."

"Who, then?" Christine asked in a voice so soft that he felt rather than heard her say the words.

He became absolutely still. "You are in mortal danger from me."

THIRTY-FOUR

"I wish you could read my mind, and sense my thoughts and emotions as you do with other humans," Christine was saying to Adrian sometime later that evening. They were sitting on a couch in the conservatory, beneath a date palm, the clear, midnight blue sky overhead.

"As do I," he said solemnly.

Christine sighed and sank back against the silk cushions. "It would make it so much easier. You would see what I see, know what I know. You are not a threat to me. You could never harm me. I am not in mortal danger, or in any kind of danger from you."

"You cannot know that for certain," Adrian asserted, storm clouds gathering on his countenance.

Christine did know. "I can. I do," she said, wishing she had the words to convince him, since for an ancient

Egyptian words were all-powerful. She even searched the venerable language of the Black Land that was stored in her brain, but the right words would not come.

She studied Adrian's regal profile. This was a man, a warrior, a king, an immortal, one who was living life as no other had before him. Little wonder he was skeptical that she would know something he did not.

"How do you know this to be true?" he demanded, tugging at the dress tie of his tuxedo.

She tried to explain. "Perhaps I have my own kind of magic."

"Magic," Adrian repeated, sounding more doubtful than before. "Human beings no longer believe in magic."

"Some do. I do," Christine said simply. "Magic was the most important and powerful tool in the world you came from, and that same world flows through my mind and my heart, and perhaps through my veins, as well."

He was listening.

"Maybe my magic is a form of genetic memory that has been handed down from generation to generation in my blood, in the very cells that make up the bones and muscles and organs of my body. Maybe it is part of my soul, my creative life-force, my *ka*," she said, deliberately using the sacred word of the *remetch en Kemet,* the People of the Black Land, his people, that was untranslatable in contemporary language. "According to some scientists and mathematicians, all modern humans are descended from the same small gene pool of common ancestors."

"My ancestors were kings and the sons of kings," Adrian stated arrogantly.

Christine tried not to smile. "You know this because your people were wise enough to keep a king list and inscribe it on the walls of Seti the First's temple at Abydos."

"There was also a king list in the nearby temple of Ramses the Second, but that is now in the British Museum," he said with a slightly indignant sniff. "I have seen it for myself. I also traveled to Paris to see the one from the temple of Amun at Karnak, which is in the Louvre." He turned his head. "Have you seen these king lists?"

"I have," she said. Sooner or later, most Egyptologists made the pilgrimage from museum to museum. "Humans keep genealogical charts of their families, but nothing as encompassing or as significant or ancient as the king lists."

"So you do not know who your ancestors were or where they lived three thousand years ago."

"I don't," Christine admitted.

"Then you can only guess at the source of your magic," Adrian pointed out.

"That's true." She went on to suggest, "It's also possible that there is no explanation for how I know what I know. Perhaps it simply is."

"What is, is."

"Exactly." Christine took in a deep breath and then slowly released the air from her lungs. "The important thing is I know you would never hurt me."

Apparently this was not enough to satisfy Adrian. "I am afraid for you." His face momentarily darkened. "Evil approaches."

Christine interlaced her fingers with his. "Then we will fight evil together."

Adrian was silent for a minute or two, then he said in ponderous tones, "You are a courageous woman, Christine, but courage alone may not be enough to fight this evil. This is evil as neither of us has ever known it. It is the Demon. It is the Monster. The Beast. The Eater of Blood and the Breaker of Bones."

His words sent a chill down her body from the crown of her head to the ends of her toes. It *was* evil as she had never known it. It was not an unknown, it was *the* unknown, *the* unknowable.

Adrian's voice vibrated with purpose. His eyes burned like coals. "You must have a weapon with which to fight this evil. I must give you a weapon."

He drew himself up and suddenly he seemed so much larger than life. Christine could almost imagine the twenty-foot-tall stone statues of Merneptah Seti that must be buried somewhere deep in the desert of the Black Land, standing guard at the undiscovered site of his mortuary palace. She could almost see his features carved onto a stone face, buried millennia ago in a sea of sand.

"And what is this weapon of which you speak?" she finally asked, her voice a rasp.

It was another moment before he said, "I am going to tell you my secret name."

Christine sat in stunned silence.

"That way you can protect yourself from me should I become the Danger, the threat to you," he said solemnly.

"But Adrian . . ." Christine understood the significance of what he was proposing to do. It was unthinkable. Inconceivable. Heartwrenching. She thought of the inscription she had memorized years ago on her first visit to Egypt. It was from the wall of a temple along the banks of the Nile, near Karnak:

> HAIL TO THE GREAT AND POWERFUL SETI THE THIRD, CALLED BY SOME MERNEPTAH SETI, WHOSE SECRET NAME IS KNOWN NOT EVEN TO HIS MOTHER; HORUS INCARNATE; SON OF AMON-RE; THE RESURRECTED OSIRIS; KING OF UPPER EGYPT AND LOWER EGYPT, UNITER OF THE TWO LANDS; DESCENDED OF SETI THE SECOND AND MERNEPTAH, OF RAMSES THE GREAT AND SETI THE FIRST, EXALTED BE THE GOD'S MANY NAMES; MAY THE STRENGTH OF ONE HUNDRED OXEN BE HIS, THE SWIFTNESS OF THE GAZELLE, THE SURE-FOOTEDNESS OF THE GOAT, THE CUNNING OF THE LEOPARD THAT COMES TO DRINK ALONG THE BANKS OF THE RIVER OF LIFE, UPON THIS THE FIRST DAY OF THE MONTH OF TYBI, AT THIS THE FESTIVAL OF THE TAIL.

Knowing Adrian's—Merneptah Seti's—secret name, *that name known not even to his mother,* gave her complete power over him. To her knowledge this was something a king had never done before.

But then a king had never encountered the evil that Adrian was sure he would soon be battling.

Adrian leaned toward her then, his breath stirring the tendrils of hair around her face and nape, and he spoke whisper-soft to her in the ancient language. The words burned themselves into her memory, into her heart, into her soul.

Christine swallowed hard, fighting back the tears. *"I am honored, great king,"* she responded in the same ancient tongue. Then she added in English, "Your secret is safe with me."

Christine whispered her secrets to him that night as they bathed in the rooftop pool under the waterfall.

"I've dreamed that you and I were in a lotus-filled pool like this, making love," she confided to him.

Adrian wanted to hear more. "And where was this pool?" he said, stroking her skin.

Christine smiled one of her secretive smiles and told him, "In a lush and ancient garden, of course."

"Of course, I remember now," Adrian said, smiling, and realized with amazement that he was still able to smile.

She went on. "The sun was setting and the sky was streaked with color. You were sitting on a stone bench wearing nothing but a loincloth. I was bathing. The lotus leaves seemed to help keep my body afloat as I swam among them. The air was warm and the water was warm, and, yet, when I glanced up and saw you watching me, my nipples hardened into small morsels of fruits, tender fruits, sweet fruits, as you later whispered to me."

"I have always been something of a poet-king," Adrian said, taking her breasts into his hands and admiring the fruits of his labor.

Christine smiled at him invitingly. "You also called lovemaking a ritual 'water dance,' and muttered something about the crocodile and its mate."

"We could learn much from the crocodile," he murmured against her flesh, pressing his lips to the exact spot above her heart. "They have survived for millions of years on this earth of ours. Few creatures can claim the same."

Christine reached down and gently grasped a fistful of his hair and brought his face up to within a single breath of hers, arching her back as she did so and wrapping her other arm tightly around his neck. "I want you to make love to me as you did in my dreams," she said, her eyes alight and burning into his.

"Yes," Adrian said, brushing his mouth against hers, touching her lips and teeth and tongue with his own.

"I love the taste of you," she whispered as she took a small bite of him.

"I love the taste of you," Adrian echoed. Then he buried his face in her hair. "By the gods, I love the smell of you."

"And I love the smell of you," she admitted.

He breathed in deeply and held her scent in his nostrils, in his throat, in his lungs, savoring it, not wanting to let it go until he was finally forced to exhale out of sheer necessity.

He had never smelled a woman like her. It was partly the scent of the ancient oil that always seemed to cling to her skin and it was partly her natural essence: an element far more elusive and difficult to describe.

"I love the way you feel," she divulged as she reached beneath the water and touched him, tracing the shape of him from the sensitive tip of his erection to the thatch of thick, dark hair.

He entangled his fingers in her chestnut-brown hair, then dipped into her to assure himself she was damp on both the outside and the inside. She climbed onto his lap and spread her legs, and he drove into her with a single, sure stroke.

Her eyes opened wide; she gazed into his. "We've done this before."

"In your dreams?"

She exhaled. "Yes."

"And in mine," Adrian said as he began to move inside her.

She was breathless. "This is better than a dream."

"Yes." He plunged deeper, ever deeper, and after a moment touched that innermost part of her.

"You will always be in my dreams," Christine said in a soft hush, in that split second before she pressed her lips to his and gave her cry of release into his mouth. Adrian took hers in and gave his own into her keeping. Then they lay back in the warm water, floating side by side, and staring up at the stars overhead.

Adrian realized he had a single prayer: That her dream would not become a nightmare.

THIRTY-FIVE

The woman was headstrong.

Christine not only wouldn't leave him or Las Vegas, she had actually moved into his penthouse. She had shown up yesterday morning, bags in hand, unpacked her things—not that there was much to unpack; he'd have to convince her to do some shopping downstairs, on a house account, of course—and had summarily taken over one of his closets. Her toothbrush and toiletries had suddenly appeared on the shelf in the master bath, next to his own grooming items. Lacy undergarments dangled from the hooks beside the shower. And the sheets on his bed smelled of that wonderful and unique scent that was Christine.

The woman was headstrong, but he wouldn't have her any other way, Adrian admitted to himself as he stared out the window of his office, several floors below the penthouse suite.

It was a rare overcast day in Vegas, with storm clouds on the horizon. He wondered if a sandstorm was kicking up somewhere out in the desert.

There was a discreet knock on his office door.

"Enter," he said in a commanding voice.

"There is someone here to see you, sir." The speaker was his personal secretary, Ms. Runyon, an efficient woman of indeterminate years who respected his position, knew everything there was to know about Las Vegas, and had the rapier-sharp mind of a world-class trial lawyer, which she had once been. Ms. Runyon was discreet, formidable, nobody's fool, and suited Adrian perfectly. He paid her well. In fact, better than most corporate executives, which suited her perfectly.

"Who is it, Ms. Runyon?"

"Two men, sir. The gentleman who appears to be in charge says he's a detective with the LVMPD." Ms. Runyon glanced down at the crumpled business card in her hand.

"Show them in," Adrian instructed.

"Do you want me to remain present as an attorney, sir?"

"That won't be necessary, Ms. Runyon. The sheriff of Metro and I are old acquaintances."

"Mister King," came a gruff baritone. "I'm Detective Charles Osborne."

Adrian said, "Detective."

A thumb was hooked over Detective Osborne's right shoulder. "This is Detective Frank Miller."

Adrian acknowledged the second man with, "Miller."

Miller nodded his head and proceeded to look

around the executive suite as if he had never stepped foot into the upper echelons of the corporate world before, which was no doubt true. It was also doubtful that Detective Frank Miller recognized the two Rauschenberg works of art on the wall he was presently staring at, or the Jackson Pollack on the wall opposite it.

"We're with Metro homicide, Mister King."

He listened disinterestedly.

"We've run into a bit of a mess, sir. The body of a young woman was found early last week in a Dumpster."

Adrian waited. He had learned a long time ago that waiting was something he was very good at and something that human beings were very bad at it.

"The thing is, Mister King, the victim apparently had sexual relations with a man shortly before she was killed."

"Sadly, Detective Osborne, these things happen even in Las Vegas." Crime was a part of any big city, including Sin City, Adrian reflected. Although the LVMPD worked diligently to keep the streets as clean as possible since everyone's livelihood depended on keeping the tourists safe and happy.

Osborne raised one beefy hand and rubbed the back of his neck. "What makes this case a little different, sir, is the fact that every drop of blood had been drained from the female victim's body."

Adrian went still.

Osborne went on to explain in more graphic detail. "There were puncture marks on her wrists, her neck, even on her breasts, which were implants."

Adrian tried to react as any normal human being would. "Puncture marks? Was she a user?"

"Not that kind of puncture. These marks were more like someone had sunk very sharp teeth into her veins and drank every drop of her blood." Osborne shook his head as if he thought he had seen everything in his days as a police officer and had just found out he was wrong. "Except for the ones on her breasts—those were more like tears or rips, like whoever did it to her was angry when he found out they were fake."

Adrian knew the detective was going to get to his point sooner or later.

"At first we assumed it was her boyfriend, a guy named . . ." The detective glanced over his shoulder to the officer behind him, who was still staring at the Rauschenbergs.

Miller immediately supplied the name. "Jason Stanford-White, with a hyphen."

Osborne swung back. "Does that name ring a bell, sir?"

Adrian shook his head and made certain that absolutely nothing changed: not his breathing, not his posture, not even the pupils of his eyes. He had been trained from boyhood. He had fought face-to-face battles with the enemy. He'd had a long time to perfect the methods a warrior learned to conceal his reactions.

Besides, no mortal casino owner would recall the name of a guest who had gambled at his establishment a week or two ago. Even if that guest had won a large sum of money.

"It seems Jason Stanford-White played blackjack here at the Royal Palace and won some pretty big bucks."

Adrian shrugged.

"Probably doesn't seem like a lot of money to you, sir. But we understand he walked away with nearly three-quarters of a million."

Adrian made sure his voice contained just the right rational tone. "I think anyone would consider that a substantial sum, Detective."

Osborne nodded several times as if he were in agreement with Adrian. "We got that information from the motel where Jason Stanford-White and . . ."

Detective Miller supplied another name. "Candy Adams."

". . . and Candy Adams were staying. Apparently Jason asked the motel manager to place the check from the Royal Palace in his safe. Said he wasn't allowed to cash it if he valued his life." Osborne let out his breath on a long, drawn-out sigh. "At the time the motel manager thought Jason was kidding."

Adrian arched one dark brow. "I'm afraid I don't see where this is going, Detective Osborne."

"Oh, didn't I say?"

The policeman was a clever man in his own way, but Adrian could still read him like an open book.

Osborne continued. "Normally the first person to fall under suspicion when a woman is found murdered is the husband or boyfriend. So we went looking for Mister Stanford-White."

"Did you find him?"

Osborne nodded. "Jason picked up a plain brown envelope at the motel's front desk a couple of days ago and then proceeded to use the money to settle his bill before checking out. The manager says he caught a glimpse of what was inside the envelope: a wad of brand-new one-hundred-dollar bills."

Adrian waited for the other shoe to drop.

"Then last night Jason Stanford-White's body was

discovered in an alley behind a crack house. He'd been dead for at least a day or two. Maybe longer."

Adrian shook his head. "A sad ending. Spending all that money on drugs."

"By special request, the pathology report came back pronto on this one. It says there were no drugs in Jason's system. But what's stranger than that, his blood had been drained from his body in the same way as Candy Adams's . . . with one major difference." Osborne paused, maybe to catch his breath or maybe to deliberately create an impact when he finally said, "His heart was missing."

Adrian's head came up. "Missing?"

The detective nodded. "Yep. Missing. Gone. Vanished. It had literally been ripped from his chest. I've been asking myself if it's a case of a bizarre ritual. A serial killer. A major psycho?"

Adrian could tell the man was finally going to tell him why he'd come to him with this story.

"We found this by Jason's body." Detective Osborne turned and held out his hand. Miller dropped something into his partner's palm. Osborne opened his fingers. "It looks a lot like the ring you wear, sir."

Except his ring was on his hand, of course. "May I see it?" Adrian wanted to find out for himself if the gold ring set with a bloodred scarab and inscribed with hieroglyphs was real or fake.

"Sure, why not? We've already had it fingerprinted. There were no prints, by the way. It had been wiped clean."

Adrian took the heavy gold ring and held it up to the light. He took his time and examined it carefully, but he would have known the ring anywhere. Just as he instantly recognized the name carved within the cartouche.

He made certain no signs of recognition showed on his face or anything had changed about his manner as he handed the ring back to Detective Osborne. "It's similar to mine, but I suppose there are a lot of similar rings out there."

Osborne didn't come right out and disagree, but he did say, "Funny thing about this ring, though. We asked an expert to look at it and he said it's the real thing."

Adrian frowned purposely. "The real thing?"

"It's a real Egyptian antiquity," the officer said. "Since everybody in Vegas knows you're a collector of this stuff, we were wondering if anything is missing from the collection here at the Royal Palace."

Adrian volunteered, "There are hundreds of items on display in the lobby and in the art gallery downstairs. Doctor Henry Davis is a renowned Egyptologist and our in-house expert on these matters. Believe me, if anything is missing he'll be the one to know."

"You don't mind if we talk to this Doctor Davis?"

"Not at all." Adrian raised his voice a fraction. "Ms. Runyon?"

She instantly appeared in the doorway. "Yes, Mister King."

"Would you call Doctor Davis and let him know that Detective Osborne and Detective Miller will be coming down to speak with him in a few minutes?"

"Of course, sir."

Adrian turned back to the two men. "Is there anything else I can do for you gentlemen?"

"Thanks, but we've taken up enough of your time," Osborne said as they walked toward the door. He turned back and said, "By the way, the sheriff sends his regards."

"You tell the sheriff he still owes me fifty bucks from the last time we had a fund-raiser in my wine cellar," Adrian said, and they all laughed as if the detectives understood the joke.

Once he was alone again, Adrian immediately called for Ra- hotep. "We have a problem, General," he said, once the head of his security had walked into his office and closed the door behind him.

Rahotep always kept his ear to the ground. He considered it his sacred duty. "The police were here."

Adrian got straight to the point. "There have been two recent killings. A man and a woman have been found with all of the blood drained from their bodies. The man's heart was missing."

Rahotep's eyes narrowed in thought. "Do you suspect an Eater of Blood?"

Adrian nodded.

"Do you know who it is, my lord?"

Adrian frowned. "I've examined the ring they found next to the man's body." He suddenly felt sadness, sadness and rage beyond anything he had ever felt in his entire existence. "I recognized the name inscribed within the cartouche. It was Seth."

Rahotep's hand went to his side as it would have gone to his sword in the ancient days. His face was a study in controlled fury. He spit the words out like a curse. "The traitor."

Adrian braced himself and said the words aloud. "The traitor is here in Las Vegas."

THIRTY-SIX

It was a stormy night with dust and wind swirling into Las Vegas from the desert. There was heat lightning on the horizon, brittle pieces of jagged light that split the sky for an instant and then instantly disappeared. The air was thick with a sense of foreboding. The atmosphere was ominous, dark, gothic.

Adrian and Christine entered the salon. There was a bottle of Pol Roger on ice as he had instructed, and two crystal flutes on the table beside the sofa. Next to the champagne glasses was a tray of chocolates, dusted with gold leaf and imprinted with Adrian's initials. He had the chocolates imported from Belgium; they were the finest money could buy.

Unfortunately money can't buy everything, he reflected, acutely aware that his wealth couldn't buy him peace of mind, or guaranteed safety for Christine, or even a future for himself.

"Is there anything else you require, Mister King?" Rahotep said from his post beside the door.

Adrian glanced in the general's direction. "That will be all for tonight, Rahotep."

"Then I wish you and Doctor Day a good evening," the head of his security said as he backed up a step or two military fashion, turned, and exited the salon.

"Will you have a glass of champagne with me, Christine?" Adrian asked, popping the cork on the bottle.

"Yes, thank you." she said, accepting the crystal flute. "Does the general ever call you anything but Mister King?"

Adrian was determined to be sociable, tonight of all nights. The last thing he wanted was to alert Christine to the heightened danger that surrounded them. "Sometimes if we're alone and he's certain we won't be overheard, Rahotep will refer to me as 'my king,' but usually in the ancient language."

"Like that first night when we were in the eagle's nest," Christine mentioned.

Adrian lowered the glass in his hand. "Ah, so you did catch that. I thought you might have."

Her expression was benign. "At the time I told myself that it must have been a slip of the tongue. Or perhaps I'd simply heard General Rahotep incorrectly. I was very conscious of the fact that Bryce St. Albans was making a fool of himself."

"St. Albans wasn't—isn't—your responsibility. The man is a liar, a braggart, and something of a fraud." Adrian shot her a deep frown. "I don't even think he's much of an Egyptologist."

"Let's just say that Bryce doesn't have a lot of original theories of his own." Christine seemed to stop herself from saying any more.

"You speak too kindly of the man." Adrian knew his tone had been disapproving. He quickly tempered his comment with, "Your kindness, however, is commendable."

Christine made a small gesture with her glass of champagne. "Are we celebrating something?"

"Yes," Adrian said, but she need not know it was a celebration born of desperation. He would have preferred to send her away, but she would have none of it. So he must protect her here in his hotel, in the world that he had created, to the best of his ability. He had given her a weapon: his secret name. But the danger had doubled. He had extra security assigned to every part of the Royal Palace. It was a matter of sitting and waiting: the calm before the storm.

Christine was obliging. He knew she sensed something wasn't right. She always seemed to know. "What shall we drink a toast to?" she said, a little too cheerfully.

Adrian put on his mask, the one he usually assumed at social functions. "How about a toast to the past, the present, and the future?" he suggested.

"You have a past, you currently have a present, but I can't promise either of you a future," said a disembodied voice from the open doors to the patio beyond.

A young man stepped out of the shadows and into the light. The stench that came into the room with Seth was pungent, overpowering, nauseating. He smelled of rotting flesh.

This was the impending threat he had been sensing

for the past few weeks, Adrian realized. It felt like the gathering storm clouds that lead to a fierce and violent display of lightning and wind and driving rain. It was the killing desert when buzzards circle a pathetic carcass and pick at the last hank of flesh or hair or miserable bone. The feeling had been growing stronger and stronger since the night Candy Adams and Jason Stanford-White had been in his casino, the same night Adrian had first smelled the ancient oil and had first met Christine.

"Good evening, Father." Adrian heard a sharp intake of air from Christine.

He was incensed. "How did you get in here?"

"Does it matter?" Seth said and shrugged nonchalantly.

His son wasn't quite a man, but he was certainly no longer a boy. Adrian assessed him at a glance. Seth was dressed like an adult in an expensive hand-tailored tuxedo, but there was no growth of beard on his face or chin. There was, nonetheless, something very old, something very ancient, and something very evil in his eyes.

"Let's just say I have my ways," Seth said in a silky tone. "I've learned how to use the nighttime to my advantage, and I've perfected the art of concealment."

Adrian wasn't feeling sociable. "What do you want?"

Seth made a pretense of being offended. "What, not even an offer of a glass of champagne to the prodigal son returning to his father? Or a small morsel of sweet chocolate?"

Adrian didn't say a word.

Seth hummed under his breath. "What do I want? What do I want?" he repeated several times as he circled the salon, spreading his stench wherever he went and leaving it on everything he touched.

He must maintain control of his emotions, Adrian warned himself. The idea of revenge was so tempting, so sweet, and he could easily take his revenge now. But he knew that Seth would never have come here without a plan.

What was the traitor's plan?

It couldn't have been a coincidence that Seth had killed the young couple who had been gambling in his casino several weeks ago. It wasn't an oversight that the cartouche ring so similar to his own was left at the murder scene, or that the police would somehow link it all to him. Seth must feel safe coming here or he would not expose himself to the others who had awakened.

"What do I want? I want what I've always wanted," Seth finally announced. "I want you dead." Then he shook his head from side to side. "You just won't die, will you, Father?"

Adrian was brusque. "I did die."

Seth laughed; it was a dark, soulless sound. "How stubborn of you not to stay dead then, and how inconvenient for me."

Inconvenient? Is that what his life, his death, and his rebirth were to his firstborn?

Adrian was succinct. "Why?"

Seth seemed perfectly willing to tell him. In fact, he seemed to *need* to tell him. "I wanted to be king, of course. I wanted the power and the privilege and the wealth of the pharaoh." He sniffed. "And I had no intentions of waiting around like the sons of the Great Ramses waited. Twelve died while their father lived on and on into old age. It was only the thirteenth son, by then middle-aged himself, who finally took his rightful place as god-king."

Adrian's expression tightened. "You were my first-born son. You would have been the heir to my throne."

Seth stopped and confronted him, his king, his own father, the man he obviously considered his enemy. "When? You were always the bravest and the strongest of any man in the Black Land. When would I have inherited your throne, Father?"

Adrian refused to answer the question.

Seth obviously preferred to supply his own answer. "When I was too old to enjoy the 'pleasures' of the harem? When I was old enough to be supplanted by one of my siblings?" Anger flashed across the once handsome, now contorted features. "We both know you always had your doubts about me. Once Mother was gone, you intended to pass over me in favor of one of my younger brothers. Or even one of your own brothers. How many did you have?"

"My father had a dozen sons," Adrian stated.

"And I knew there were a dozen others you would rather see sit on the throne of the Black Land than me." Seth's mouth twitched in what might have been a smile; it was a terrible sight to behold. "So I decided not to take any chances. Besides, I wanted power sooner, not later."

"You always were impatient," Adrian said, an unexpected edge to his words.

"Yes, I was," Seth agreed. "But I have learned patience since my awakening."

Adrian shook his head. "Frankly, I didn't think you had the stomach to pull off an assassination."

Seth stiffened. "In some ways, Father, you always did underestimate me."

"Perhaps," Adrian said. Then he added, "I did not read your name on any of the king lists."

He knew for a fact that Seth was absent from the history books. His name had not been etched into any monuments, temples, or lasting remnants of their once-great civilization. And although it had been millennia ago, much of his own legacy—the legacy of Merneptah Seti—had survived.

Seth gave the matter some thought. "Perhaps because I had no son to come after me, to honor me, to make certain my name was preserved for posterity." Then he made a profane gesture and chortled under his breath. "Of course, I did try to destroy your name and your legacy, I admit it. I even plotted to have your body hacked to pieces and scattered as fodder for the carrion-eaters and the donkeys, but I was prevented from doing so by some of your loyal henchmen."

Adrian knew he must keep Seth talking. If his son—the word sent a chill down his spine—was distracted, Adrian might have a chance to develop a plan of how to deal with this foul killer. "How long did you live after I was murdered?"

"Not long enough, *Father*." Seth said the word as if it were a curse.

"You had accomplices." It was a statement, not a question.

The salon filled with cruel laughter. "Maya was the instrument I chose for your destruction. It seemed fitting somehow that someone so devoted to you, someone who loved you, someone who was above reproach in your eyes, someone whose loyalty to you was unquestioned, could be forced to betray you."

"Maya has been here to see me."

"Yes, I know," Seth said slyly. "I smelled her desperation. She must be turning and is fighting the inevitable, just as for once you're fighting something that is greater and stronger than yourself. Something not even you can overcome."

Adrian did not have to ask if Seth had overcome the hunger, the thirst, for human blood; it clung to him like a haze of red horror. "You are already an Eater of Blood and a Breaker of Bones," he said, unable to keep the disgust from his voice.

"I had no choice," Seth said in a petulant tone as he strolled across the salon and took the glass of champagne from Christine's hand, his fingers brushing against hers. He threw his head back and drank it down in a single gulp. "Excellent vintage."

Adrian was amazed to see that Christine did not falter during the unexpected and repulsive contact with Seth. She did not recoil in fear. In fact, she stood her ground, her gaze unwavering. He was very proud of her, he realized, for the awful stench must be overwhelming to her as well.

"Why did you have no choice?" he asked his firstborn.

"Because I awakened as an Eater of Blood and a Breaker of Bones. In fact, the first humans I consumed were robbing my tomb, so it was no less than they deserved."

Adrian stated clearly, "You killed them."

Seth was equally adamant. "I did what was necessary to survive." He raised one hand and examined his fingernails, admired them, didn't seem bothered in the least by the fact they were long and sharp and stained with blood. "Besides, they were expendable."

"How many have you murdered?"

Seth made an airy gesture with his obscene fingers. "Heavens, I no longer count."

"Was there no other way for you to survive?"

"I don't know," Seth said, shaking his head. "I enjoy feeding the hunger. I've never wanted to find an alternative."

"You murder innocent people," Adrian said wearily, his heart weighed down with the enormity of what his eldest son had become: an Eater of Blood and a Breaker of Bones, a demon, a *vampire*.

Seth smiled, and it was a smile that sent a shiver along even Adrian's flesh. "I only take the weak, the inconsequential, the ones no one will miss," he said as if that were all the justification his actions needed. Not that he seemed to feel the need to justify himself.

"You're playing God," Adrian said with all the condemnation he could muster.

"I thought we *were* gods, Father." As Seth circled the room again, he chastised, "Or have you decided that you're human, after all? Has love transformed you? Do you love the human woman?" He paused in front of Christine and drew one long, razor-sharp fingernail down her cheek, leaving a tiny streak of oozing blood behind. "Shall I show you how to sink your teeth into her neck and drain the life essence from her body? Shall I show you what I have become? What you will become?"

"You always were weak," Adrian said, passing judgment.

"You consider it weakness. I think of it as strength. The strength to take what I need, what I want, as befits those of us who are immortal, those of us who are as far above these frail, inconsequential humans, as they are from a mere ant that crawls on the ground."

Adrian's voice was that of the king he had once been; the king he hoped always to be. "I will not become an Eater of Blood. I will not allow myself to become a creature of the night, a monster, a vampire who feeds on human beings."

Seth snorted and drops of a pale watery liquid ran from his nostrils. He didn't bother to reach into his pocket for a handkerchief, but wiped it off with the sleeve of his tuxedo jacket. "You're already a vampire. You feed on their thoughts and their emotions. That's what has kept you alive all these years."

"It's not the same thing." By the gods, it wasn't. Seth—he could not bring himself to call this abomination his son any longer—was wrong, but he also was right.

Seth taunted him. "It won't be long now and you will be powerless to stop the hunger. It will become a craving so intense that it will be all you can think about and all you can feel. You will want it more than life itself. And in the taking, you will continue to live."

"At what price?" Adrian asked, feeling as if he were already fighting for his sanity, his soul.

"The price is irrelevant. How do you intend to stop the lust for blood? I see it in your eyes. I smell it on your skin and in your hair. Your hunger grows, Father. The temptation to feed grows. Once you cross over, you will possess a strength and a power that you can only now imagine." Seth's voice was soft and seductive.

"No!" Adrian roared, bringing his fist down on the table at his side. There was a resounding *crack* that filled the room and echoed off the walls. The table wobbled for a moment and then split in two and crashed to the floor.

"You see," Seth said with an undertone of smugness, "your self-control is already slipping away. Soon you will have no choice but to feed. And we usually feed on those nearest at hand." His gaze fell meaningfully upon Christine.

"I will not cross that line," Adrian vowed. It was a sacred promise he had made to himself and to all he had ever held dear.

"You will."

"You've been waiting for just the right moment to reveal yourself, haven't you?" Adrian said, realizing it was true.

"Of course I've been waiting. Patiently, I might add. I did tell you I'd learned patience since awakening. Now the wait is almost over." Seth turned and said to Adrian offhandedly, "You did get my message, didn't you?"

Suddenly Adrian knew what he had strongly sensed all along. It was Seth who had set up the young couple, first as winners at the Royal Palace and then as his own victims.

"You don't honestly think a couple like Candy Adams and Jason Stanford-White had the money to bankroll a trip to high-end Vegas, do you?" Seth was compelled to brag. "It was so easy to read their minds and emotions, and influence their actions. Jason was a quick learner. And I must confess that I enjoyed winning something that was yours, Father, even if it was merely money. But then these humans worship money as they once worshiped the god-king, the pharaoh."

"The police were here this morning. The young couple have been found with their bodies drained of blood."

"You got the rest of the message, then." Seth slapped his thigh with delight. "I did think the missing heart was a nice touch. I've been waiting for your reaction."

It was then Adrian nearly doubled over from the odor of malevolence that emanated from Seth. His chest tightened around his heart, and his insides twisted into knots.

"Waiting," he said, lowering his voice, instilling it with all the power and persuasiveness that were his. Seth was here tonight for a reason, and the only reason he could think of was Christine. That filled Adrian with fear such as he had never known. Not for himself, but for her. Christine was not immortal. She could be hurt. Killed.

Seth was moving closer to Christine when he spoke with a pleasure that seemed to radiate from him. "I know I can't harm you by trying to kill you, Father. But I can make you suffer by watching me harm *her*." He moved so quickly it was a blur, and then there was a dagger at Christine's throat. "It would be so easy for this knife to slip and cut her jugular, wouldn't it? She would bleed to death and there wouldn't be anything you could do to prevent it."

"You must not harm her." Adrian fought against the temptation to charge across the room. "If you must feed on someone, let it be me."

"What would be the pleasure in that?" Seth said, sounding almost sane for such an insane creature. "I want to see your eyes as I drain the life from her. That will make it all the sweeter."

"Don't do this, son."

Seth laughed and it was a terrible sound. "So now you call me son." Bitterness dripped from his voice as surely as blood would drip from his dagger.

Adrian had to try again. "Take me in her place. I'm the one you hate, the one you've always hated. Kill me."

Seth paused and said, "I thought I had a long time ago. Killed you, that is."

"Why did you hate me so much?"

"*Did?* I hate you now as much as I ever have. Hate is the strongest emotion I have ever felt. Hate has kept me alive. It has given me strength when I might have otherwise failed. Hatred is a wonderful thing, Father," Seth said as his fangs began to emerge from his mouth.

THIRTY-SEVEN

Christine felt her heart beating within her breast like the wings of a dove fluttering haplessly in the death grip of a hawk's beak. But she wasn't afraid for herself. She was only afraid for Adrian. He was the one who must stand helplessly by. She knew if he were the one with a dagger pricking his jugular, she would have gladly given her life to save his.

Perhaps that's what she was doing.

Seth reeked of evil. His face was close to hers. She could smell the sickeningly sweet aftermath of human flesh on his breath.

Christine understood now why Adrian feared becoming an abomination like his firstborn son had. What an unholy and unthinkable ending it would be for the last great ruler of ancient Egypt, Horus incarnate, son of Amon-Re, the resurrected Osiris, the strongest and the wisest and the greatest pharaoh of them all: King Merneptah Seti.

What an infinitely sad and loathsome existence it would mean for the great man Adrian King.

Seth suddenly drew back an inch or two. "I've just remembered something. In all the excitement I'd forgotten the best part," he said, seemingly delighted with himself.

With his free hand he dug around in the pocket of his tuxedo jacket and removed an object. Christine couldn't see what it was.

Seth focused his gaze on Adrian. "I may be younger than you are, Father, but you always were as swift as a gazelle and as strong as an ox. And I don't trust you even with my dagger pressed to the woman's throat. You may not care for her as deeply as I have surmised. You may prefer your revenge over her life." Seth tossed a metal object in Adrian's direction.

Adrian caught the metal contraption. "Handcuffs?" he said, frowning.

Seth chortled. "Not just any handcuffs. These were crafted by a gifted metal worker once employed by a regime, which sadly for him, is no longer in power. I believe he used to specialize in making instruments of torture." Seth shrugged indifferently. "Maybe he still does. Anyway, this particular pair of handcuffs is ten times stronger than the standard police issue. I think they should be sufficiently constraining to thwart even you, Father."

Immovable and unmoving, Adrian simply held the handcuffs in his grasp.

Seth offered a possible reprieve. "Perhaps I won't

kill her if you obey me, Father." Then he barked out his orders. "First, you will wrap your arms around the pillar beside you. Then you will secure the handcuffs until I hear the locks click into place. Oh, and be sure to face this way. You'll want to have a good view of the events about to enfold before your very eyes."

Adrian went very still.

"Do it now," Seth said, pricking Christine's neck with the dagger. She could feel something wet trailing down her skin.

Adrian reluctantly handcuffed himself to the marble pillar. This was a king who had never taken orders from anyone, let along this aberrated creature who was of his own flesh and blood, Christine thought, gazing at the man she loved. And she did love him, she realized.

"I am not afraid, Adrian." She was surprised by how calm and serene she sounded.

Adrian kept his gaze fixed on hers all the while, looking straight into her eyes, into her very heart and soul, and she was once again swimming in a blue pool, their lotus pool, and she was warm and free, safe and loved. She clearly saw the two of them, and then she heard the laughter of a child. A golden-haired child. How odd, a child had never been in any of her waking or sleeping dreams before.

Fragments of a song, an ancient lullaby, came to Christine. She closed her eyes and began to hum under her breath. Then, as if in a trance, she started to sing softly in the ancient language:

You are my child, my golden child, golden like the sun.
You are my child, my silver child, silver like the moon.

You are my child, my firstborn child, you will never
    know fear.
You are my child, my beloved child, your mother is
    always near.
You are my child, held safe in my arms,
    Sleep now my child, sleep.

Christine heard a clatter and quickly opened her eyes. Seth was staring at her with horror and bewilderment on his features.

He fell back a step. "What kind of trickery is this?" he demanded to know.

"Trickery?" She didn't understand.

His voice quaked. His hands shook. His whole body was shuddering. "How do you know this song?"

Christine felt as if she were awakening from a dream. "I don't know," she said. "I simply do." She wetted her lips and told him, "I've always remembered the ancient time, things and places and people that I can't explain. I believe it is my magic."

"Magic," Seth repeated, his eyes bulging from their sockets, capillaries bursting one after another, red against white. "It is the lullaby my mother sang to me when I was a child." He recoiled; his fangs retracting. He spoke in the tongue of the *remetch en Kemet*: *"You are She-Who-Is-Feared. You are the Soul Gatherer."*

THIRTY-EIGHT

This was the chance he'd been waiting for, Adrian thought as he watched the dagger slip from Seth's hand and drop to the floor. He must find the strength to break his bonds before his son recovered from the shock, retrieved the knife, and began his butchery.

There was only a small window of opportunity, a few precious moments in which to act. Seth was totally focused on Christine. He had forgotten about his father, forgotten about his hatred, about his thirst for revenge, which was as unrelenting as his thirst for human blood.

Adrian closed his eyes and opened the floodgates deep inside his mind, calling upon his strength, his determination, his magic, and his power. Without a sound, he chanted ancient words in an ancient tongue: Words of the warrior, words of the king, words of the vengeful gods, words that brought down both blessings and curses upon the land and its people.

He could feel himself filling with primal strength and primal urges. He sensed he was teetering on that fine line between man and beast. His body tensed. His muscles burned. He could hear blood gushing through his veins and arteries to every part of his being. He could feel sinew and bone and muscle infusing with adrenaline. He skin seemed too small, too constricting to contain his body mass. It was almost as if he must shed his outer skin like a snake and expose a newer layer underneath.

Whatever the cost to himself, it was of no consequence, Adrian thought. He would do this for Christine, just as she had been willing to give herself up to save him.

He focused on the handcuffs. He envisioned they were weakening, that the metal was becoming heated, soft, malleable. He sensed the alloy failing. He was nearly there.

Sweat broke out on his skin. Blood vessels bulged. Muscles flexed with effort.

The metal gave way.

His hands were released.

He was free.

Adrian swept across the room then like the wind, like an invisible force of nature. He seized both of Seth's arms and pinned them behind his back.

"No!" Seth cried out, caught off guard, imbued with sudden rage, struggling against his father's superior strength.

"It is no use," Adrian said with utter finality. "It is finished. It is done."

"It will never be done," Seth hissed as his fangs began to appear. His malevolent gaze fell upon Christine. "It is her fault. She is the demon who would steal my *ba*, my shadow, my *ka*, even my name."

These were the rants of a madman. A killer. A thing that had once been human, but was no more.

Adrian looked at Christine. "Can you go to the door and call for Rahotep?"

"Yes," she said, her voice oddly tremulous.

As soon as her back was turned, Adrian raised his fist and brought it down like a mighty hammer on the back of Seth's neck. The creature slumped to the floor, unconscious.

He would not soon awaken.

"I do not know how the traitor was able to slip through our security," Rahotep said to him a few minutes later. "It is my responsibility and my fault, my lord. I have failed you."

Adrian wearily shook his head. "Seth has his own kind of power, General. Evil often does. All the security measures in the world may not keep evil out if evil is determined to get in." Then he turned to Christine. "I want a doctor to look at those cuts and scratches. Meanwhile, hold this against your neck," he said, wetting a napkin and pressing it into her hand. "You appear to be a little pale."

"I feel a little pale," Christine admitted, leaning back against the nearest chair.

"I think you'd better sit down," Adrian suggested. He noticed that for once she decided to follow his advice.

"What will you do with . . . ?" Christine seemed unsure what to call Seth.

"We will deal with the traitor according to the old ways," Rahotep stated, without explaining what the old ways were.

"No police?" It wasn't really a question on Christine's part, but more of a confirmation.

"No police," Adrian confirmed. "Human law enforcement does not have the understanding or the means to deal with the creature my son has become. They would label him a madman and lock him away. But we cannot take the chance that he would somehow escape and be free to kill again." He sighed. "We might not have the means to stop him next time."

"And he must be stopped," she acknowledged.

Adrian nodded. "Seth is incapacitated for now, but I must still act swiftly and decisively." He turned and said to Rahotep, "Arrange for a vehicle, General. Then, under the tightest security, transfer our prisoner from the penthouse to the parking garage." He added, "I will join you shortly."

"It will be done, my lord."

Once he was alone with Christine, Adrian found he had so much to say to her and no time in which to say it. "You were very brave this evening," he said, taking the damp napkin from her hand and gently wiping a streak of blood from her cheek.

"So were you."

That made Adrian smile. "I am expected to be brave."

Christine gave him a watery look. "So am I."

Adrian was filled with wonder and with regrets. But he would only express the wonder to her. Regrets were best left unspoken. "You are an extraordinary woman, Christine, and the most courageous person I have ever known."

"And you are the most extraordinary being I have ever known," she said, pressing her hand to his lips.

"You will be safe now," he said.

"And what about you?" she asked, shadows forming in her gray eyes.

He knew his face didn't give anything away. "I must deal with Seth while I can."

"Then I will be waiting for you when you return," Christine said simply and confidently.

Adrian stood and did not speak again until his hand was on the doorknob. Then he whispered one word and one word only in the ancient language: *"Beloved."*

"You cannot come with me this time, Rahotep. There are other duties you must see to," Adrian said as he climbed behind the wheel of the vehicle.

Rahotep was at a loss to understand. "But, surely, I must be by your side when you deal with the traitor."

Adrian shook his head. "There is something more important that I need you to take care of."

"What is it, my lord?"

"You must stay and protect Christine Day." Before Rahotep could react, he went on to say, "Those are your orders, General."

Rahotep stood tall. "Yes, my king."

"Don't tell her where I am going or why I do not return until it is over." Adrian looked out at the night sky. The storm had passed. There was a sliver of moon, and stars were appearing. "There will be a bright sunrise in the morning, Rahotep."

"Yes, my lord."

Adrian reached out the window of the vehicle and clasped the other man by the hand. "Farewell, my old friend."

THIRTY-NINE

"Why did Seth fear you?" Rahotep asked Christine after the doctor had thoroughly examined the scratches on her face and neck, given her a tetanus shot, and bid her goodnight.

Christine was restless; she paced back and forth in front of the salon doors that opened onto the terrace. "He thought I possessed the ancient magic, that I was a demon, the Soul Gatherer."

Rahotep's eyes widened. *"She-Who-Is-Feared?"*

She nodded. "Apparently Seth was convinced I intended to take the five elements of his existence from him: his *akh*, his *ba*, his *ka*, his name, and his shadow."

Rahotep's mouth curved into a humorless smile. It was one of the few times Christine had seen any expression on the general's usually stoic features. "I would like to have seen the traitor afraid, if only for a moment," he said.

"Thank goodness a moment was all Adrian needed to break free of the handcuffs. I'm not sure Seth would have remained afraid of me for long," she ventured.

"Sometimes all a warrior requires is the time it takes to draw a single breath, and the battle may be won or lost."

Christine stopped and regarded the man seemingly intent on keeping her company throughout this long night of waiting. "You and Adrian—Merneptah Seti—have fought many battles together."

This time it was Rahotep who began to pace back and forth. "Yes." The general was a man of few words.

"Can you not fight this final battle with him?" She knew she was almost pleading.

Rahotep came to a sudden halt and turned to face her. "I would give my life to be by his side, but he will not allow it."

"Do you always do as he commands?" Christine gave a dismissive wave with her hand. "I'm sorry. Of course you do. You must. You have given your solemn oath, and you have sworn your allegiance to him as your pharaoh."

"And as my cousin and as my friend," he said, making their unique relationship clear.

Christine was getting that feeling in her gut again. "There is something you are not telling me, Rahotep."

He avoided eye contact with her. "What makes you say that, Doctor Day?"

She knew it! Something wasn't right. In fact, something was very wrong. "Did you know the small lapis lazuli jar is missing from its case in the master suite?"

Rahotep cleared his throat but did not answer her question.

"Then you did know," Christine concluded. "Adrian has taken it with him, hasn't he?" It was a rhetorical question that required no answer. The man would refuse to give her one, anyway. She asked another question. "Why isn't he back? He should have returned by now." She went and stood at the terrace doors and stared out into the night. "Where has he gone, Rahotep?"

"I cannot say."

"Cannot or will not?"

"One is the same as the other if a soldier has been given his orders," he stated.

Christine turned and faced him head-on. "Exactly what are your orders? Can you tell me at least that much?"

Rahotep considered her request. Then he drew a breath and straightened his already ramrod-straight shoulders. "My orders are to watch over you and protect you."

She hesitated only briefly before saying, "That is most considerate, but I do not need to be watched over. Nor do I need to be protected. I am in no danger."

"How do you know this?" Rahotep inquired, showing rare curiosity.

"Because I can feel it, sense it. I know it," she explained, without really explaining.

"Perhaps the traitor was right at least in this. Perhaps

you do possess some of the ancient magic," the general said, regarding her with newfound respect.

Christine suddenly had to know. A feeling of urgency drove her to speak. "What is Adrian doing with Seth?" She kept asking questions and pressing for answers. "What did you mean when you said we will deal with the traitor according to the old ways? Where has Adrian taken his firstborn? Why has he been gone so long? Where is he?"

Rahotep went and stood at the open doors of the salon. He looked out at the night sky. "The weather is clearing. There will be a bright and fierce sunrise on the morrow."

Christine opened and closed her mouth on a barbed retort. Was Rahotep trying to tell her something without breaking the sacred oath he had sworn to his king? "Adrian has gone to meet the rising sun." She made it a simple statement.

"He has."

Finally! She had found a way of getting answers without asking questions that compromised Rahotep's integrity—at least, according to his code of honor.

Christine tried again. "Adrian is allergic to sunlight."

"He wasn't always. That has only become a problem since he felt the hunger growing stronger."

"He fears becoming a Eater of Blood."

Rahotep sighed heavily, wearily. "All of those who awaken live with this fear."

She tried to think quickly, clearly. "If Adrian, who has not completely turned, is allergic to sunlight, then Seth, as an Eater of Blood, will find the presence of the sun-god Re fatal."

"The traitor will die," Rahotep stated, without any show of sentiment.

Christine was starting to get that awful feeling in the pit of her stomach again. "And Adrian?"

There was only silence . . . like the silence of the tomb.

Christine reached out and placed her hand on the general's arm. "You must tell me, Rahotep." She swallowed her fear and the threat of tears in the same breath. "He did not say good-bye to me."

"What words could my lord hope to find in any language to say good-bye to you, my lady?"

Christine's heart was drumming in her breast. "I am his destiny, Rahotep. He has dreamed of me for three thousand years and I have dreamed of him all my life. I am his, and he is mine. We live or we die together. If our king has gone out to meet the sunrise, then I must be at his side." Christine instilled all of her magic into the words she was about to say, for devotion and loyalty were concepts that Rahotep had lived by every day of his existence. "You must take me to him. It is your duty and it is my destiny."

Rahotep faced her squarely. "He has taken the traitor out into the desert."

"Do you know where?"

"Yes."

"Then you must take me to him."

Rahotep looked out at the night sky. "We must hurry if we are to reach them before the rising of the sun."

FORTY

In his final act as a father and as a king, Adrian carried the still-unconscious Seth out into the desert.

He left his vehicle at the foot of the mountain where he had hoped to build a home one day—a day that would never come now—and walked for a mile or two until he reached the middle of nowhere.

To the east, as far as the eye could see, there was nothing but sand, low scrub, a few scattered boulders, and more sand. It reminded him of the desert of his youth. The ritual, the calling down of the purifying fire, was best performed with only the desert around him.

Adrian reached the place where the rising sun would first strike the earth and placed Seth on the ground at his feet. Then Adrian made certain that the lapis jar was secure in the breast pocket of his jacket. The ancient repository had long contained his spirit, his magic, his power as god-king. It could not be left behind. It must go into oblivion with him.

With the dawn still a promise on the horizon, Adrian began the ritual blessings, the recounting of his lineage as far back as recorded history and then farther back to the time when that history was told and retold around campfires and in the tents of his ancestors.

He recited the prayers of forgiveness and the appeals to the gods for mercy.

He spoke the spells from the *Book of the Dead*, asking the ferryman for a swift journey into the East. He addressed the Keepers of the Gates, acknowledging that he knew them and their names. He related the spell for sailing in the Great Bark of Re and for passing over the circle of fire. He asked to be transformed into the phoenix. He requested that his heart be weighed in the scales of balance and against the feather of righteousness, and that his heart not be taken from him.

He gave the litany of the gods, reminding them that he would remember to lift his face to the sky so that he would be permitted to see the sun-god Re.

Then Adrian began his personal farewells. "May the Eye of Horus be the protector of Rahotep, who has long watched over and protected me," he said aloud.

Was that the first light of day on the horizon?

He took a deep breath and continued. "May my brother, Prince Rekhmire, be spared from knowing the Hunger and awakening as a damned soul."

There was a streak of pale color against the dark sky.

Adrian raised his eyes. "Above all else, may all that

is good, all that is honorable, all that is beautiful be a part of Christine's life, and may she live long and well."

The darkness was swiftly disappearing, consumed by the light.

Adrian could feel the cold night of the desert being replaced by the heat of the coming day. Soon it would be a blazing sun and a fiery heat; it would become the purifying flame, the sacred fire that would cleanse him, cleanse Seth, and both father and son would go to that place where they could never harm anyone again.

Then he raised Seth up and wrapped his arms around his firstborn. His sadness gave way to acceptance. "Those with evil in their hearts will be consumed. So it has been written; so it must be done."

Adrian closed his eyes for a moment and called upon the power within him to bring forth the sacred fire from the rising sun. He could feel the first of the licking flames touch his skin. He opened his eyes and beheld the light of day.

FORTY-ONE

They raced across the desert, racing against time and the rising sun, leaving a thick cloud of dust behind them.

Christine felt a sense of urgency in every fiber of her being. "We must hurry, Rahotep!"

"I know, my lady. I know," he said, never taking his eyes from the dirt road in front of them.

Christine could smell dust in the air, taste it in her mouth, feel it settle on her skin even with the windows closed. There was dust behind them and to either side, stirred up by the tires of their four-wheel-drive vehicle. "How far is it now?"

"Not far."

"How far is not far?"

Rahotep scowled.

Christine's stomach was churning. *Too* far. "Is that the sun on the horizon?"

"Yes," Rahotep said through tight lips.

"What will happen when the sun has risen?" She had to know. She must know.

Rahotep swerved off the dirt road and headed across the desert at breakneck speed. "Merneptah Seti will call down the sacred fire, the purifying fire."

Fire was not considered a force for good to an ancient Egyptian. Fire meant that the body was consumed, utterly destroyed, and then there was no hope of ever entering the afterlife.

Christine's heart clenched. "What will this sacred fire, this purifying fire do?"

"It will consume all those with evil in their hearts," Rahotep stated, pressing his foot down on the accelerator until they were almost flying across the desert floor.

Christine was thrown hard against the seat belt secured across her chest. She grabbed hold of whatever she could and held on for dear life. "It destroys evil."

"Evil must be destroyed," Rahotep said, his gaze fixed on the barren landscape ahead. "There is no other way."

"He cannot be evil," Christine whispered. She could never love evil, and she loved Adrian.

"Adrian King is still a great warrior and a great king. He will not allow himself to become evil," Rahotep stated without a shred of uncertainty in his voice.

"There is the sunrise," Christine said, her spirits flagging just for an instant.

Rahotep leaned forward over the steering wheel as if

that would somehow make the vehicle go faster, although he had already gunned the accelerator to the floor. "There may still be time."

Please let there be enough time, Christine prayed. Then her head came up sharply. She pointed toward the east. "What is that in the desert?"

Rahotep's eyes followed her line of vision. "The sacred fire," he said.

"It's blue," she said, her eyes opening wider.

Rahotep made a movement with his head that resembled a nod. "I know only what I have been told and what I read long ago in the sacred texts. Once the purifying fire has been called down, it will burn until evil is devoured, until it is completely consumed and utterly destroyed. The fire burns both hot and cold. The fire knows no mercy. There is no recompense and no escape from its flames."

"Seth is doomed."

"The traitor has been doomed since he took the wrong pathway a very long time ago."

"There may still be time to save Adrian," she said, and in expressing her hope aloud she believed it was possible.

Rahotep retreated into silence.

"The fire seems to be burning brighter, bluer," Christine said as Rahotep slammed on the brakes. She fumbled with the catch on her seat belt, broke free at last, opened the passenger-side door, and began to sprint across the desert floor.

Christine ran faster than she had ever run in her life. She ran until she was gasping for air. She ran until her muscles cramped with pain, until it felt like sharp knives were piercing her flesh. She ran until she felt certain she would collapse and could run no more. And yet she knew she must run faster still.

She was close enough now to see that Adrian was holding an unconscious Seth in his arms. There was no expression on his face. His eyes were closed, as were the traitor's.

She skidded to a halt ten or fifteen feet from the flames. She could feel the fire's icy heat even from this distance. There was no time to catch her breath. She opened her mouth and forced the sound from her lungs. "Adrian!"

There was no reaction from either figure encompassed by the fierce blue fire.

Christine tried again, harder, louder this time. "Adrian, I am here!" she cried out.

Adrian stirred. His eyes slowly opened. It was as if he had been sleeping, dreaming. His gaze was unfocused for a moment. Then he turned his head, slowly, looking at her with his endless blue eyes. She saw recognition dawn on his weary features. "Christine, you should not have come."

She stood her ground. "I had to," she said, her heart beating hard and fast in her breast.

"It is too late," Adrian said, resigned.

"It is not too late," she argued, fighting for his life; fighting for her own as well.

"I must leave you."

"No." It was a protest, a plea, a prayer, all in one simple word.

He seemed to force himself to speak, as if the effort was almost too much for him. "Yes."

Her heart knew what her heart knew. "Wherever you're going, I'm coming with you," Christine stated.

Adrian's features twisted in pain. "You don't know what you're saying."

"I do know." Christine stepped several feet closer to the flames; it licked her skin like freezing heat.

"But I must go into oblivion," came the hoarse confession from Adrian.

"Then I go into oblivion, as well." She took another step toward him. "I'm not staying here without you."

"Why?" The word was torn from the center of his being.

"Because I love you." Christine felt the power in her words. She knew the words rang true like a clarion call on this sky blue morning. "I love you more than life itself."

Adrian's pain seemed to increase. His face was distorted with the pain. "I can't let you die."

"You can't stop me."

She knew he could hear the absolute certainty in her voice. She had never loved a man as she loved this man. For the first time she understood that it was the two of them together alive, or it was the two of them dying and going into the void, into oblivion, into whatever was on the other side of the blue flames, side by side.

"But it will all be for nothing if you die," he said in a voice distorted by anguish.

"And it will all be for nothing if *you* die, my love," Christine cried out, her blood standing still.

Adrian set his jaw. "I have no choice."

"Yes, you do. You can choose life. You can choose to be with me." She was a warrior, fighting a battle as life-threatening or as life-preserving as any battle he had ever fought as the great warrior-king. "You must let Seth go into oblivion without you. You must give him up to those who wait for him."

There was infinite sadness on Adrian's face. "Whatever he has done, whatever he has become, Seth is still my son."

Tears were thick in her own throat. "I know. But he has taken many innocent lives. He became evil, and his soul is damned unless you allow him to be purified by the sun god Re."

Adrian's face was a study in torment.

"Please, Adrian. You must let him go."

Christine thought she saw Adrian waver for a moment. If only she could find the words to make him understand; words that would carry the power to sway him.

"Beloved," he murmured as if in farewell.

Then Christine found her voice and her power in the ancient language, *"You have waited for me, beloved, for thousands of years. I have waited for you all of my life. Stay with me now that we have finally found each other."*

Christine watched as Adrian absorbed the power of her will, her words. She knew he was about to step out of the fierce blue fire and return to her.

Then the unthinkable happened.

Seth opened his eyes.

FORTY-TWO

Adrian felt a slight movement in the unconscious body he held in his arms. He could tell from the startled expression on Christine's face and from the one of alarm on Rahotep's that Seth was awakening.

His son stirred. Although he was as limp as a rag doll, Seth raised his head and looked around for a moment. He could not stand on his own. He could not speak. He did not know where he was or what was happening to him. He was still held in the grip of that other time and place created by the ancient rituals.

He could do this for the man, for the prince, he had once hoped that his firstborn would become, Adrian vowed.

He whispered into Seth's ear. "I will go with you, my son. I will be at your side. I will not allow you to go on this final journey alone. The first face you beheld at your birth, the person who loved you most in life, will be the last face you will see at the end."

Adrian could feel something give way within the creature and within himself. It was surrender. He felt a sense of peace washing over them both.

He raised his eyes to Christine's. *Good-bye, my love,* Adrian thought, but he did not say the words aloud. If he went quickly, swiftly, without warning, she would not be able to follow. He would die. But she would live.

It was then Christine drew near the fire and started to sing a version of the ancient lullaby:

> *You are her child, her golden child, golden like*
> *the sun.*
> *You are her child, her silver child, silver like the moon.*
> *You are her child, her firstborn child, you will never*
> *know fear.*
> *You are her child, her beloved child, your mother is*
> *always near.*
> *You will be held safe in your mother's arms.*
> *Sleep now.*
> *Forever sleep.*

Seth closed his eyes again and, as the purifying flames took him, the last word on his lips was, "Mother."

Then he was gone, consumed, cleansed, dust to dust, and ashes to ashes.

The blue flames were extinguished. The wind calmed to a desert breeze.

FORTY-THREE

Adrian found his arms were suddenly empty.

Seth was gone.

Yet he was still alive.

It took a minute or two for that to sink in. He had been prepared—resigned—to go into oblivion, into nothingness, to leave behind all that he held dear, to give up his life in order to remain the warrior and the king he had always been, to sacrifice himself so that Christine might live and live free of any fear, any danger, any evil he might become.

Why was he still here? He should have been consumed by the sacred fire, the purifying fire.

"Those with evil in their hearts shall be consumed. So it is written; so it must be done."

He had awaited the sunrise. He had recited the rituals

and the litanies and the history of his family. He had invoked the spells from the *Book of the Dead*. He had said his personal farewells. He had stood within the circle of the sacred fire. He remembered feeling the flames licking at his flesh, his bones, his muscles, every part of his body. He had done all that was required of him and then he had waited to be taken.

Yet the blue flames had been extinguished. The purifying fire had gone out. And he had not been consumed or devoured or destroyed. He had not disappeared. He had not vanished.

He was still here.

Adrian stood in the bright light of a new day and he felt the sun's warmth on his skin. It did not burn him; it simply took the cold from his body, an icy coldness that seemed to have penetrated right through to the heart of him.

He raised his face to the sky and took a deep breath. His mind felt strong and clear, just as his body felt strong and clear.

Adrian looked within himself and he no longer sensed evil. Could the evil be gone? The monster? The demon? The thing within himself that had been so close to becoming an Eater of Blood? Was it all gone? Vanquished? Had he entered the light and somehow left the darkness behind?

He had told Seth that the person who loved him most in life would be waiting for him. And, at the very end, Seth had called out to his mother.

Who would be waiting for him? Who loved him the most in life? Then he heard Christine say his name. "Adrian."

He turned and saw that she was standing a foot or

two from him, waiting, watching him with eyes filled with love. "Christine."

The power of that one word brought her rushing into his arms. She wrapped hers tightly around him and pressed her face to his chest as if she needed to hear the beat of his heart, as if its steady rhythm would reassure her that he was truly alive and well.

"For a moment there I was afraid I was going to lose you," she mumbled against the lapel of his jacket.

"For a moment there you nearly did," Adrian said, amazed that he was standing in the middle of the desert, the sun a blazing yellow orb high in the sky, and he was feeling intact, whole, in fact, *healed*. He felt more like himself than he had in a very long time.

Christine put her head back and gazed up into his face. "What happened?"

Adrian shook his head. "I'm not certain."

The words tumbled out of her mouth. "One minute you were both engulfed in blue flames and the next Seth was gone," she said, her voice filled with wonderment.

Adrian slowly nodded. "I heard you singing the ancient lullaby to him."

"It seemed the right thing to do," Christine said, holding on to him as if she would never let go.

Adrian realized he was finally at peace with Seth's fate. "I want to believe that he is with his mother again, that she will always care for him and perhaps even love him."

"Sometimes a mother can love a part of ourselves even if it is only a memory of the innocent child we once were."

Adrian gazed down into the face of the woman he loved. "How did you become so wise?"

Christine smiled at him with a Mona Lisa smile. "That's part of the magic of being a woman."

Christine had watched as first bewilderment, then astonishment had spread across Adrian's face when the sacred fire, the purifying fire had burned out, leaving him behind. Intact, alive and well, and breathing.

She had stood there, her pulse racing like the wind that swept across the desert, creating swirling dust devils in its path. She had not been able to move or speak or even think. She had been frozen in place, as if an icy hand had touched her for an instant and she was no longer living flesh and blood.

Then she had felt the sun warming her from the inside out, suffusing her with its heat and its light. And the first word formed by her lips had been *Adrian*.

Now she was safe and warm within his embrace, and Christine knew she would never be cold again.

Adrian took a half step back and patted the pocket of his tuxedo jacket, now covered with a fine layer of dust. "It's still there."

"What is?" Christine said, trying to brush the dust from his face, his beautiful face.

Adrian reached into his pocket and took out the small, ancient lapis lazuli jar. "You see, don't you?"

Christine wasn't sure that she did. "See?"

"My spirit, my magic, my power are intact as well." Then Adrian laughed. He actually laughed. A deep masculine laugh of satisfaction; a joyous sound.

"Of course they are," Christine said, not the least bit surprised. It would take more than a wild blue fire to destroy the great king that would always be inside this man, this very special man.

Adrian wiped the sleeve of his jacket across his forehead, leaving a streak of mud behind as dust combined with the sweat forming on his brow. "It's hot out here."

Christine bit away the amused smile that wanted to form on her mouth. "Of course it's hot out here. We're standing in the middle of the Nevada desert. The sun is beating down on us. There's no shade in sight. And, according to the weather reports, the temperature is supposed to hit one hundred degrees today."

"That would explain it." Adrian shrugged off his jacket and rolled up the sleeves of his shirt. "Look at that," he said, pointing to his bare arms.

"What?"

"It's been a long time since I've felt the sun on my skin," he said with wonder.

Christine felt tears in the back of her throat. She swallowed hard. The man she loved had been willing to sacrifice himself for the sake of others, for her sake, and in giving up his life, he had been given back his life.

She had always wanted to believe that love was stronger than hate, that good triumphed over evil. It seemed that it had. Then something she remembered from the old days, the days before Adrian—or had it been in one of her dreams?—came back to her as if in an ancient memory: *If you believe completely, it becomes your truth.*

Christine took Adrian's arm and started toward the vehicle she and Rahotep had left a short distance away.

Adrian looked around, puzzlement written on his handsome features. "By the way, where is Rahotep?"

Christine answered his question. "Despite some discomfort from the sun, the general is walking across the desert to retrieve the vehicle you left at the foot of your mountain." She paused and brushed her lips across his. "I also think he wanted to give us some privacy."

"Smart man," Adrian said, after he had kissed her thoroughly, raising the temperature in the desert by at least another ten degrees. Then the king stopped dead in his tracks. "Rahotep disobeyed my orders."

"You mustn't blame Rahotep for bringing me here." Her tone was uncompromising. "I made him tell me where you had gone. I forced him."

Adrian put his head back and laughed. "You forced him? Rahotep is the strongest and toughest soldier I have ever known."

"Ah, but I have my ways of dealing with even the strongest and toughest, my lord," she stated.

"And what might that be, my lady?" Adrian asked, bringing his face down close to hers again, finding her mouth with his.

When Christine had finally caught her breath, she said, "Well, in your case, beloved, it's magic."

FORTY-FOUR

Adrian King stood on his mountaintop, gazing out over his domain. It had been only a few months since that fateful day in the desert, and yet sometimes it felt like a lifetime ago. Perhaps because his life had changed in so many ways during these past months, in ways he could never have imagined.

He heard Christine grumbling as she walked up behind him. "Well, the landscape architect is convinced I'm insane," she said, sounding slightly vexed.

Adrian turned and slipped an arm around her waist. "And why is that?" he asked.

She gave an exaggerated sigh. "It's the lotus pool."

Adrian tried not to smile. He knew how important it was to Christine to include a lotus pool in her plans for the home they were building on this mountaintop, the home he had always dreamed of.

"The man claims that a lotus pool isn't practical in the desert," she explained. "I informed the gentleman that lotus pools were often found in deserts."

Adrian made sympathetic noises.

"The wretched man insists that he knows best and that all the plants will die. I informed him they will not die. Then he had the audacity to inquire why I was so confident since he was the horticulturist and I was the Egyptologist." She blew out her breath expressively. "I confess that I told him an outright lie."

That caught Adrian by surprise. If anything, his wife was honest to a fault. "You lied to him?"

Christine nodded. "I told him that I had *the* green thumb to end all green thumbs."

"What did he do then?"

"He threw up his hands and said, 'Fine, a lotus pool it is,'" she admitted, with no small amount of chagrin.

Another battle won, Adrian thought, reveling for a moment in one of the mundane and myriad details of everyday life that he would not have appreciated until recently. So many of the battles he had fought had been a matter of life and death. "I'm sure it will be the perfect lotus pool."

Christine looked up at him and laughed. "You don't care one bit about a lotus pool, do you?"

"That's where you're wrong," he said, dropping a kiss on her mouth, then lingering when her seductive taste enticed him to linger. "I intend to put that lotus pool to very good use."

"Now you're reading my mind," she said, wrapping her arms around his neck.

"You know, that continues to baffle me," Adrian said.

"I can read everyone else's mind, but I still can't read yours." He slid a hand down her back and cupped her derriere in his palm.

"I'm not so sure about that sometimes," Christine murmured as she pressed her body into his. They could both feel the consequences of the physical contact between them: His erection was hard and fully burgeoning between them.

"Have the landscape architect and his minions left yet for the day?" he asked, suddenly wanting to be alone with Christine, knowing there must be someplace in this house under construction where he could make love to her without peril of splinters or nails.

"I'm afraid not," she said softly against his lips. "But you'll be the better for waiting."

"The better for waiting?" Adrian almost roared, incredulous.

"Of course, you're already very good at what you do," Christine said, teasing him, backing away from him, and finally taking him by the hand.

"And where do you intend to take me in this state?" he inquired with a telling glance down at the visible bulge in his pants.

"There's a nice private area in that small grove of trees that was planted last month," she pointed out.

When they reached the secluded spot, Adrian slipped his jacket off and spread it out on the ground. "Your seat, my lady."

Christine smiled graciously and sat down on his coat. "Thank you, my lord."

Adrian settled beside her and leaned back against the trunk of one of the larger trees that had been transplanted. "These workmen seem to take their own sweet time getting things done around here."

His comment obviously amused Christine. "This isn't the construction of the Great Pyramid," she said with what sounded suspiciously like a chuckle. "We don't have an endless supply of labor willing to work for bread and beer."

"Maybe that's where we're making our mistake. Maybe we should be paying them in bread and beer," Adrian said, almost serious. "There was a lot to be said for the old ways."

Christine suddenly appeared pensive. "Do you miss the old ways very much?" she asked.

Adrian drew a deep breath and straightened his shoulders. He stared at the desert landscape that extended as far as the eye could see. "It was good to be king." Then he focused his attention entirely on the beautiful woman at his side. "But it is *very* good to be Adrian King."

Christine's hopeful smile said it all. "No regrets?"

"How could I have any regrets?" he said, running his fingers through her silky chestnut-brown hair with its fiery red tones highlighted by the sun. "My dream finally came true. How many men or women can say the same?"

"I can," she whispered, turning and pressing her cheek to the hand caressing her hair. Then she looked up at him, and gray eyes—eyes the color of the sky as evening fell upon the ancient land—searched his. "You won't live forever now."

"Trust me, eternal life isn't all it's cracked up to be," Adrian said sardonically. "Some things come at too dear a cost. A long human life span is a small price to pay to not to become an Eater of Blood, a lonely, soulless creature, a vampire."

Christine shivered beside him. "What of Maya? Or of Rahotep? What of the others who may have awakened and whose fate you do not know?"

"I am their king. I am the head of the ancient and royal house of Merneptah Seti. It is my duty and my responsibility to lead them, to rule them, to protect them, and, if necessary, to punish them." Adrian smiled coldly. "I may be all that stands between the monsters and their innocent victims."

Christine interlaced her fingers with his. "I will stand guard beside you. Whatever small gifts, whatever magic I possess, I will use to help your people and my people."

"*Our* people," he said, emphasizing the first word. "From this day forward we stand together."

"And we will win this battle," she said confidently.

Adrian loved the determined look Christine got on her sweet and intelligent face when she made perfunctory statements. "How do you know?"

She wasted no time in telling him. "That day in the desert you won the eternal battle between good and evil, and, in the process, you healed yourself. Who but the greatest warrior and the greatest king could perform such a feat?"

Adrian knew it was true. "But I was only able to do so with your help."

Christine disputed his claim. "I didn't do anything to help you. I stood helplessly by, hoping and praying."

Adrian disagreed with her. "You showed me what love is, what love could be, what it should be. You showed me that love is believing when everything tells you you're a fool for believing. Love is the strongest and most powerful emotion we can feel, and the only emotion I will ever need now." He brushed a strand of hair from her face. "Love is eternal. Love is forever. That's what you taught me."

Christine's hand flew to her mouth. "I was wrong."

Adrian frowned and looked down at his wife, puzzled and a little startled. "You were wrong?"

She nodded. "You will live forever."

That got his attention.

"We will live forever," Christine said, looking up at him with truth shining in her eyes. "Don't you see? We will live on through our children and their children and their children's children, as far into the future as we once looked into the past, until this present time becomes their ancient time. That is our destiny."

And it was her destiny to love and to be loved by this very special man, Christine thought as she sat beside Adrian under the shade of the only stand of trees on the mountaintop.

His hand strayed to her breast as he sat and seemingly stared at the horizon. Her body responded instantly, as it always did. She swatted at his hand as if she were shooing away a pest or a buzzing insect. "Someone may see us," she said out loud, knowing full well that no one was within earshot.

"I don't care if they do," Adrian said with a surprisingly cavalier attitude.

"Well, I do."

"I'm teasing you, wife. I watched as the last construction crew drove off in their pickup truck five minutes ago. We are quite alone now on our mountaintop."

Christine frowned and vowed she would make him pay . . . in the most delicious ways, of course. "You have just recently learned how to tease me, husband."

"Perhaps, but I do think it was another lesson I picked up from you." He laughed and added, "Beloved."

Christine pushed him onto his back and pinned him to the ground with her body, her knee pressing into his thigh, making sure his erection was precisely where she wanted it, and knowing full well that Adrian could flip her over with one hand tied behind him. "Perhaps there are other lessons to be taught *and* learned about teasing," she said, as she began to slowly unbutton her blouse.

Adrian reached out to help her undress, to touch her, to caress her. She swatted his hand away again. "You may look, my lord, but you may not touch."

Then Christine proceeded to divest herself of her clothes until she was stripped down to a small pair of silk panties. Adrian had watched her all the while, his eyes turning darker and darker blue, his erection, hard and distended, pressing against her inner leg, so near and yet not near enough.

"I can see I am a rank amateur when it comes to teasing," Adrian admitted, licking his lips.

"Even the wisest among us may still have a lesson or two we can learn," she said, feeling the heat radiating from Adrian's body as if he had stored up warmth from the desert sun all day.

Christine leaned over and traced his lips with her

tongue, delving in just there at the corner of his mouth, and there where his lips parted slightly. "You taste of tartness and the sweet grape that goes into the finest wine." She took another lick, this time extending it to his neck and then lower to where she began to unbutton his shirt. "You taste of something male." She moved lower, unzipping his trousers, and catching him as he sprang free. She took him into her mouth, lathing him with her tongue, tasting him, testing him, flicking the tip of his erection, gently nipping on his flesh, scarcely coming up for breath. "Oh, yes, you definitely taste of something very male," she teased, her voice pulsating with passion.

Oh, how little she had known of passion before this man. And no one had felt passionate about her until this man. No one had ever loved what she was in her heart, in her mind, in her soul. There was love and passion in the way she kissed Adrian and in the way he kissed her.

With her nearly nude body flattened against his from breast to thigh, she could clearly feel the outline of every bone, every muscle. Only the thin material of her panties separated their flesh. There was no doubt about the state of his sexual arousal: He was about to explode.

"I think today's lesson on teasing is concluded," Adrian said through sexually tensed lips, flipping Christine over and quickly divesting himself of his clothes. "I'm going to kiss you until you can think of nothing but my kiss. I'm going to touch you in places where you've only dreamed of being touched. I'm going to make love to you until there is nothing but the two of us and our bodies are so intertwined that we can't tell one from the other," he said, his voice a husky promise of passion.

He ran his hand along her shoulders, then skimmed her bare breasts, teasing her until her nipples were begging for relief. He began to lick her with his tongue, nibble on her with his teeth, and suckle her with his mouth until Christine was quite certain she would go insane from the sensual torment.

Then just when she thought she could take no more, Adrian reached between their bodies and his fingers found her warmth, her silky damp flesh, that throbbing nub. He brought her to one climax after another until she cried out his name on a sob.

"Please, Adrian," she pleaded. "Please, my love."

He took pity on her and himself. He drove into her with a single, sure thrust of his hips. Then he moved into a hard, rhythmic surge, thrusting deeper and deeper into her until she couldn't breathe, couldn't think.

Then she heard his hoarse shout and felt him thrust into her one final time, emptying himself into her, wringing himself dry, filling her to the brim, calling her name over and over, "Christine. Christine. Christine."

This was where she belonged, Christine thought as she floated in the aftermath of making love with the man she loved and who loved her. She could spend forever in Adrian's arms. . . .

AFTERWORD

◪ For most of my life I've been fascinated by ancient pharaonic Egypt, specifically what is known as the New Kingdom dynasties (approximately 1550–1069 B.C.E.), especially the Eighteenth and Nineteenth dynasties. Among the fabled rulers of this time period are Tutankhamen, Seti I and II, and Ramses II, also known as Ramses the Great.

I have meticulously researched this period in Egyptian history, including the details of embalming and burial for a New Kingdom pharaoh, but I'm not an Egyptologist. I'm a storyteller, and at times I've granted myself poetic license for the sake of that story.

In addition, I've employed some modern terms that the ancient Egyptians would not have used. For example, the king did not refer to himself as *pharaoh*, although others could have beginning with the New

Kingdom dynasties. Pharaoh is the Greek form of the ancient Egyptian phrase *per-aa*, ("great house"), and was initially used to refer to the royal palace.

The *Book of the Dead* is also contemporary terminology. The ancient Egyptians referred to the funereal texts as the "spell for coming forth by day," because the several hundred spells (or "chapters") and incantations included supposedly insured that the deceased would live again after death.

They also believed that the body had to be preserved for the next life. This was the reason for their elaborate embalming rites and the creation of mummies. The worst of all fates was to have your body cremated, for then there was no hope of rebirth. In fact, the punishment for the most heinous crimes was to have your body burned and your ashes scattered on a road where you would be trampled underfoot by both people and donkeys.

The "seven sacred oils" is another modern-day expression. By the Eighteenth and Nineteenth dynasties, there were actually nine or ten ceremonial oils of importance. They would have been spoken of as simply "the oils," with names like *seti-heb* (odor of festivals) and *hekenw* (odor of praising). There were not distilled perfumes, but oils scented with herbs and spices. Most of the plants from which these ancient oils were derived have not been accurately identified, nor have the oils been re-created.

Names and spelling are another variable. Each pharaoh had five names. The two by which the king was most commonly known were called his "cartouche names," and included the name he was given at birth.

That is the name I have used for Merneptah Seti. I have also chosen to use Seti, rather than Merneptah, as his personal name. (In addition, Seti would not have been referred to as Seti III in ancient times. The kings were only numbered in recent history.)

As far as spelling, I've simply chosen what appeals to me most: I prefer Re to Ra; Seti rather than Sety. Note: Tutankhamen is also spelled Tutankhamun.

The ancient Egyptians described their land as Kemet, which literally translates as the "black land," because of the rich deposit of silt left behind by the annual flooding of the Nile. They called themselves *remetch en Kemet* or the "people of the black land."

There are still amazing finds yet to come in the Valley of the Kings and elsewhere in what was once the Black Land. It is estimated that nearly one-third of ancient Egyptian monuments have yet to be found, including the tomb of the most beautiful and famous queen—Nefertiti.

Last, it should be noted that the poetry, invocations, papyrus writings, and the character of Seti III are all of my own creation.

AUTHOR'S NOTE

Music speaks to me. It always has. One of my earliest memories is of playing on the swing set in the backyard of my childhood home and singing "Somewhere Over the Rainbow."

When I was seven, I begged for piano lessons. At sixteen I wanted to be a singer and studied voice. At twenty-one (realizing I wasn't headed for stardom on the Broadway stage after all), music lessons were nudged aside and I had to earn my living as a high school English teacher. At twenty-six, I started writing fiction, and the rest, as they say, is history.

I love many types of music from classical to Celtic, opera to rock. Music affects and reflects my mood. I choose different music for each book—not to listen to as I write, but to listen *before* I write. Music transports me to where I need to go emotionally as I sit down at my computer each day. It gets me "in the mood" and serves as a kind of emotional shortcut.

For those interested in knowing what pieces of music I was inspired by while writing *Night Life* (all my personal favorites), they are listed below, classical composers before their music; popular performers, when specifically mentioned, after the song title.

"Sometimes I Dream," Mario Frangoulis

"Who Wants to Live Forever," Sarah Brightman

"Wicked Game," Chris Isaak

Puccini's "Nessun Dorma," from *Turandot*

Grieg's "In the Hall of the Mountain King," from the *Peer Gynt Suite No.1, Op.46*

"Holding Out for a Hero," Bonnie Tyler

"Miserere," Andrea Bocelli, featuring John Miles

"This Could Be Heaven," Seal

"Dreamer," Bethany Dillon

"Pretty Vegas," INXS

The score to *The Phantom of the Opera*

Dangerous, immortal, and thirsting for blood.
Like it or not, "they" are among us.
Laurell K. Hamilton
the Anita Blake series
MaryJanice Davidson
the Undead series
Christine Feehan
the Dark series and the Drake Sisters series
Diane Whiteside
the Blood series
Charlaine Harris
the Sookie Stackhouse series
Don't miss the best in vampire fiction from Berkley.
penguin.com